Those
Lazy, Hazy, Crazy
Days of Summer

MARK DAYDY

Cover design by Mike Daydy

ISBN: 9781076349934

CONTENTS

Prologue:

Island of Dreams

#10. Lorraine Sherwood

Posted 17 years ago

Wow, lots of lovely comments about the old days. I was actually looking for photos of Sandy Bay in the 60s and 70s when I found the tourist authority website's noticeboard by accident. Imagine my joy when I saw a thread entitled 'Memories of Hopton's Holiday Camp, Sandy Bay.' I worked at Hopton's for ten seasons, '67 to '76. Does anyone remember Ralph, Lenny, Don and Eddie or any of the girls: Josie, Helen, Carol, Georgie, Julie, Ronni and Diane? Eddie and Josie were an item for three summers – a record for Sandy Bay! It seems so long ago now, but the memories will stay with me forever.

Freddie Archer replied 17 years ago

Hello Lorraine. Freddie here. I went to Hopton's in Sandy Bay as a 12-year-old boy in 1959. I loved it. At 22, I auditioned to become an orange coat. I wasn't chosen but I did get a job doing other duties at the camp for two seasons. I recall you and many others. Sandy Bay was certainly a special place – one big (mostly) happy family, all working hard and making our way in life. I remember Georgie singing Those Were The Days after the comedian had been on. What a great voice! I wonder how she is. It would be wonderful to catch up with old friends.

*

It was a Tuesday evening in March and there was work to do – enough to keep Laura Cass occupied until bedtime. No surprise there. Since taking a job in the education training sector, she was often busy, working beyond her regular hours into the evening and weekend. That's why the last thing she needed was for her mother to leave a large cardboard box with her an hour ago.

No, actually, the last thing she needed was to open the box, remove the contents – an ancient projector and tripod screen – and set the thing up.

Laura didn't know why she'd engaged with the last thing she needed. She didn't have time for it. All the same, she had already dimmed the lights and switched the projector on.

That's probably why she was transfixed.

In bright sunlight, the 1966 olive green Ford looked impossibly new as it cautiously approached the ferry's boarding ramp. Laura's mother, Bev, then ran, still filming, to the car to get back in with Laura's father, Jim. There was a glimpse of him laughing and probably saying "turn it off", although the 1960s cine film didn't have a soundtrack, so Laura could only guess what people were saying.

She moved closer to the screen, wanting to reach out and touch…

The camera panned to the rear seats where Gran was holding baby Laura. Laura's older sister, Mandy, was wedged between Gran and Grandad, who was singing. He often sang.

The camera came round to her dad again, driving the car forward, and bumping onto the ramp and into the belly of the boat. Yes, he was singing too.

Watching the old cine reel, Laura, now a woman of fifty-two, felt the flickering images burning into her soul.

"I miss you," she told the smiling image of her father.

The scene changed. They were aboard the ferry, which was now moving away from the dock. Laura guessed her grandad was behind the camera for this bit, because the film showed both her parents out of the car and taking in the sea view. Her dad looked immortal. Not at all like a man who would be gone within six years.

The camera panned around, perhaps too quickly, to take in the ferry's cargo – now looking like a museum of 1960s cars and fashions. Everyone looked so happy in that simple, carefree setting.

The scene changed again. It was a different part of the boat and Grandad was on bended knee pretending to propose to Gran. Laura worked out they'd been married thirty-five years by then. It was good to see the old 'uns having fun.

Then she worked out she wasn't far off their age now.

The scene changed again, returning to the forward view of the sea, the distant island, and the promise of what lie ahead.

Outside Laura's window, east of London, it was a cold 21st Century evening, with a threat of overnight snow. This couldn't have been more at odds with the warm glow of the moving images on the screen. Indeed, the pile of old 8mm cine film reels, sitting on the coffee table, was full of sunshine, thanks to her dad's insistence on filming every holiday of her early childhood.

The storage sleeve of the reel she was watching was marked 'Isle of Wight 1967'. It was one of their trips to Hopton's Holiday Camp in Sandy Bay all those years ago. Laura was so glad her mum had rediscovered them in the back of her wardrobe.

The doorbell rang.

Laura left the movie running and went to answer it – with the intent of sending whoever it was away.

"Hi!" said her daughter, Amy. "Not disturbing you, are we?"

"No, of course not. Come in, come in. I was just watching some old home movies your gran brought over."

Amy, looking weary, was holding a portable car seat containing baby Evie – a gorgeous two-month old cherub who was fast asleep. Behind them, Amy's fiancé, Ross was coming from the car parked across the short drive of Laura's semi-detached suburban house.

Laura gave Amy a peck on the cheek and showed them into the lounge, where they made themselves comfortable. It was a scene Laura was still getting used to: daughter Amy, on maternity leave from her marketing job, Amy's gym-honed tax inspector husband-to-be, Ross, and their wonderful new addition.

Laura picked up her phone and took a photo.

"Doesn't Bev look young," said Amy, spotting her grandmother on the movie screen. "Are you in this, Mum?"

"Yes, I'm there," said Laura, "but I was only six months old, so mainly asleep with *my* gran – that's Joan, your great-gran."

"I do love the look of these old films," said Amy.

"Yes, there's something magical about them," said Laura. "Don't you think, Ross?"

"You can get an app," he replied.

"An app?" Laura didn't quite follow.

"You can get an app for your phone and shoot videos that look like old home movies."

"Right, well," said Laura, "I'll make some tea."

"Actually, Mum," said Amy, "we were hoping you might be able to have Evie for a few hours."

"Of course I can. When were you thinking of?"

"About now-ish?" said Amy with a hopeful smile. "Some of our friends are going out for an impromptu Chinese meal and we thought it might be nice to go along."

"Well, of course I don't mind," said Laura, wondering how, and possibly why they were continually fitting in a procession of restaurants, paintball wars, museums, climbing, and camping – all without the baby.

"Thanks Mum," said Amy, as she and Ross got up with the clear intent of leaving immediately.

"Good job I wasn't busy," said Laura. "I might have been out and about."

"You've reached the end," said Ross.

Laura was a little taken aback by this pronouncement – she was only fifty-two! But Ross was indicating that the cine reel had finished.

"Oh right," she said, noting the loose end of the film flapping uselessly around the full receiving reel.

"Everything's in the baby's bag," said Amy. "Thanks again."

"Righto."

Laura followed them to the door to wave them off.

"Have a good time, guys," she called after them.

"Thanks Mum. We won't stay out too late."

"Maybe next time you could phone beforehand?"

"Will do."

Laura watched them drive away before closing the door.

Back in the lounge, Evie was still asleep. Laura loved the little dot of a human being, but this wasn't the first time Amy and Ross had turned up unannounced. Not that Laura minded. She wanted to help. In fact, she would have been hurt not to be involved. But she also wanted to set some boundaries.

"Well, Evie, if you're going to be asleep all evening..."

Laura thought about the work she needed to do for Angela, and then changed the reel. She was soon transported back to the sixties once more, where her dad was messing around doing a very bad Charlie Chaplin impression, which Laura adored. He would have been thirty back then. It struck her that she was now old enough to be his mother.

Families...

It could get confusing when fate colluded with certain members to make other arrangements: Dad's heart giving up unexpectedly. Jonathan walking out on twenty years of marriage...

Going way back, there had been a close-knit feel to the family – but it was a solidity that had become fractured somewhere along the way. Nobody seemed particularly close to anyone anymore. Birthday and Christmas cards, yes, but evenings out together...?

She refocused on the screen. What was Dad saying? There was too much laughter to tell. From what Mum had told her down the years, he was probably saying if they turned right, they could dodge the Isle of Wight and head straight for the Caribbean. And then he was singing. What song was it?

For absolutely no reason, 'White Cliffs of Dover' came into her head. Why? She stopped the film, rewound the spool a little, and ran it again.

'There'll be bluebirds over... the white cliffs of Dover...'

"Oh," she uttered.

She rewound the film once more and, for the first time in over forty-five years, sang along with a man she still loved as much as life itself.

It didn't last, of course. The home movies were soon back in their box and, with Evie still sleeping, Laura got stuck into the ocean of work facing her.

At one point she sighed. There were a few things that needed fixing in her life. Work wasn't the only one. Standing to stretch her limbs, she yawned and reassured herself that it wasn't an impossible task. It was just a matter of finding the time.

1

The Holiday Starts… Now!

#11. Freddie Archer

Posted 16 years ago

Hello everyone. It's Freddie here. I see it's a year since anyone has commented. Previous posts #1 to #10 were by such a lovely diverse group, from holidaymakers to former staff, all sharing wonderful memories. Let's see if we can restart the conversation. I worked in the kitchen and behind the bar at Hopton's Sandy Bay holiday camp for two seasons. I remember the hard work, the fun, and the camaraderie we had there. Those stewards and entertainers in their orange coats were a cut above us bar and kitchen staff, but we all got along famously. Any other former staff or holidaymakers with memories out there?

*

At half-five on a Friday morning in mid-June, Laura, with her phone pressed to her ear, was placing the last of her travel bags by the front door. She often imagined such moments as a prelude to a wild, romantic getaway – but it was her mum, Bev, on the line.

"Harry says have you taken your travel sickness pill?"

"I don't get travel sick. I'm not thirteen anymore. Now, have you got all your stuff together?"

"You always got sick in the old days. One time, we only got to the end of the street..."

"Please make sure you're ready. I'll be with you in twenty minutes."

"Okay love. No need to rush. I must say we're looking forward to it."

"Mum... just be ready."

Laura ended the call and took a breath. This would be their first big family holiday in ten years. She felt a little out of practice.

"Right..."

She checked her appearance in the mirror. Neat, short-ish cut for summer, lightweight blouse over jeans and trainers, and raincoat to hand – perfect for a travel day.

She was looking forward to it, even though she had a ton of work to do. In her three years working for Angela Coutts' firm, there just never seemed time for a longer period of rest and relaxation – possibly because Angela Coutts' firm consisted of Angela Coutts, Laura, and a part-time admin assistant role that no-one ever held down longer than three months. Currently, it was a vacancy.

Laura transferred her stuff into the hired Toyota people carrier outside. Her brain was fried and she needed this – a whole ten days at the seaside. Stress-free time away – bliss.

As it was, Bev had suggested a two-week break but Ross only wanted to go for a week. It was Laura who negotiated a compromise.

Almost ready to go, she went through it again. Twenty minutes to drive to Epping to pick up her mum and step-dad. Another thirty to get over to Hornchurch to collect Amy, Ross and baby Evie. Then three hours to get to Lymington for the ferry.

She just hoped her mum would be ready on time.

Then she took a calming breath.

One step at a time…

Yes, she was looking forward to it. A big dose of stress-free harmony by the sea.

Perfect.

A memory flared. She was six years old and helping her dad to pack the car for their summer holiday journey. It was excitement beyond measure. Back then, they would leave at four a.m., and she and her older sister Mandy would sleep in the car. Then, halfway there, they would stop to cook eggs and bacon on a camping stove. On some trips, there would be a second car containing relatives she usually only saw at family weddings…

Laura shook off the recollection, locked up the house and got in the oversized car.

Immediately, her thoughts raced.

Have I got everything? Credit cards, luggage, hunky guy…? Oh well, two out of three's not bad.

Yes, relaxation was the thing.

De-stressing.

Calm.

Ten days away from it all.

Her phone pinged.

It was an email from Angela.

Hi Laura
Can you fit in a few things relating to the
Croydon bookings we discussed yesterday?
Please see attachments. Just wondering if you'd
had any initial thoughts?

"None that are suitable for an email," Laura muttered as she started the car.

*

By six-fifteen, Laura was beginning to worry about missing the ferry. For some reason, once she'd loaded her mum and step-dad's luggage, they both took an age to tear themselves away from the proximity of their bathroom.

Finally, twenty minutes late, Bev emerged from her modest home dressed for a yoga class. Laura's step-dad Harry followed and locked up the house. He was wearing what appeared to be a 1930s safari outfit. Early morning sunshine reflected off both pairs of sunglasses.

A further twenty minutes later, there was a delay at Ross and Amy's – baby Evie needed changing. Although Harry muttered that it might be because Ross hadn't yet sprayed enough products on his hair and body.

They finally emerged from their small apartment block with Amy carrying Evie in the portable car seat and looking exhausted. Ross followed looking dapper in a sky blue cotton shirt, white chinos and beige suede loafers.

Once all their stuff was in the car, Laura addressed them all.

"Everyone okay?" she asked. "Ross? Amy? Mum? Harry?" She turned to Evie, asleep in the baby car seat. "That's the idea, angel."

"Let's go," said Ross from directly behind.

Laura pulled away.

"Great," said Harry, sitting up front alongside her. "The holiday starts here!"

"No, it doesn't," said Laura. "We're running late and I've got three motorways to get through."

"High seventies today," said Harry, ignoring her. He always talked in Fahrenheit, as if Celsius had never been adopted by the UK. "It could reach seventy-nine."

"High twenties," Amy informed Ross, who didn't understand Fahrenheit. "It could get up to twenty-six."

"It's thirty in Crete," said Ross. "I can't wait for our honeymoon there next year."

"I can't wait to see Hopton's again," said Bev.

"Interesting stories behind these holiday camps," said Harry. "Colin Hopton did a similar thing to Fred Pontin and Billy Butlin."

Uh-oh, thought Laura. *Lecture alert.*

"Fred learned about building camps for soldiers during the war," said Harry, sounding pleased to have a captive audience in a confined space.

"I'm sure we know all that," said Bev.

"I think Billy had already opened one before the War," said Harry, "but the army took it over. Colin Hopton, meanwhile, was a keen boy scout, so he loved big communal events away from home."

"Que sera sera…" Bev suddenly began singing. Harry had to raise his voice to be heard.

Laura calmed herself. This *was* the start of the holiday and the beginning of ten whole days of relaxation. She'd just have to get used to it.

2

The Conveyor Belt of Life

#12. Alice James

Posted 16 years ago

Hopton's Isle of Wight yayyyyy!!!! Loved it. Disco Queen 1990. I got a crown and a sash. Hey, who stole the years, lol. Bring it back, yeah, I wanna do it all again.

*

Half an hour later, they were in a long line of stop-start traffic on the M25 motorway trying to reach the Queen Elizabeth II Bridge, which would take them south of the Thames around fifteen miles east of Central London. The main feature of the traffic was the huge trucks that made Laura feel vulnerable.

"Must be a breakdown," said Harry.

"Or a bad accident," said Ross.

"It's just like the old days," said Bev.

"Breakdowns and accidents?" said Amy.

"No, the generations," said Bev. "Daughter Amy, Mother Laura, and Grandmother Bev, all plotting and planning lots of activities."

"Well, that's wrong for a start," said Harry. "Amy's the mother now and the rest of us have been shunted one place down the line."

"You make the family sound like a factory," said Bev.

"It's the conveyor belt of life," Harry insisted, "and soon someone's going to fall off the end."

Laura knew it, of course. She just hadn't let the idea come fully to the surface. It would now. Once they were all on the Isle of Wight together, it would rise up and tower over them. Her mum – evergreen, eternal Bev – was now a great-grandmother whose time with Evie wouldn't last forever.

Laura wasn't ready for that. She also wasn't fully ready to become a paid up member of the Gran Club. Yes, she enjoyed taking Evie for short periods, but she was predominately still a mother to Amy. It was just that Amy wasn't acting like a daughter these days. She was too busy being a mum. Laura wasn't complaining. Far from it. Being a gran over the coming years would be brilliant – as long as people understood that she still wanted a life of her own.

"Maybe we should have gone through London," said Ross, unhelpfully.

"I thought London would be too busy," said Laura.

"Busier than this?" said Ross.

Laura wondered why she was gripping the steering wheel so hard. They hadn't moved in a whole minute.

"Obviously I didn't know the road would become blocked," she said. "According to the road reports, it was perfectly clear when we left."

"Clear?" said Ross. "The busiest part of the busiest motorway, on a Friday morning? Seriously, Laura, the M25, M3, M27 route isn't your friend."

"It doesn't need to be my friend. It just needs to get us

there."

"It will, Mum," said Amy. "Don't get stressed."

"I'm not stressed, thank you."

"Is Lymington actually the best crossing?" said Ross. "I've heard it's better to go via Portsmouth."

I'll happily drive you to Portsmouth, Ross, and dump you there.

"I'm sure they're all much of a muchness," said Bev.

"Anyway, Ross," said Harry, "didn't I hear you had a six-hour delay at the airport not so long ago? Do you remember? When you went away with your mates while Amy was six months' pregnant? See, not all planning guarantees the best outcome."

Laura got in before Ross. "If it looks like we'll be late for the ferry, we'll rebook our ticket via the app," she said.

"They'll charge you again," said Ross.

"Not if we switch within the next two hours."

"We'll be there before then," said Amy.

"Let's hope so," said Ross. "The next ferry is bound to be fully booked."

The traffic edged forward... and then came to a halt.

"The stress of travel day, eh?" said Laura. "Just think, once we're at Sandy Bay, all this will be forgotten."

"Our boat should be arriving at the dock in an hour or so," said Harry.

"That's not helpful," said Laura.

"Oh, there's no rush," said Harry. "They have to clean up all the sick first."

"Put a sock in it," said Bev.

"I'm just saying – if you need to use the onboard loo, go straightaway, preferably before the boat sails, otherwise you'll be accompanied by the liquid yawn ensemble."

"Harry!" Amy complained.

"We're not crossing the Atlantic," said Laura. "It'll be like a millpond."

They moved forward again.

Five yards.

Ten.

Halt.

"Did you get a standard ticket?" asked Ross.

"Economy," said Laura. "They were doing a special offer."

"Right, so the economy…" Ross was studying his phone. "According to their website, that's the ticket with zero refund if you cancel."

"It was a lot cheaper."

"And now it's going to be a lot dearer."

"Not if we get there on time."

"I suggest we all pray," said Bev. "Dear Lord, please deliver us to the ferry on time… and prevent those aboard from being sick all over the place."

Ross's sigh stopped the prayer. Either that or Bev had gone into silent mode. Laura just tried to focus on the fact that she needed this break, and that she wasn't alone. Despite any Conveyor Belt of Life connotations, Bev and Harry wouldn't be up for this kind of adventure for many more years. And Amy deserved a break, too, because motherhood was draining her. There was also an undercurrent between Amy and Ross, suggesting that something wasn't quite right there. To think her daughter and Ross would be getting married this time next year…

They crept forward again.

Five yards.

Ten.

Halt.

"We used to stop in the old days," said Bev. "We used to pull over onto the roadside and fry up bacon and eggs.

Do you remember, Laura?"

"You still can," said Ross. "The car in front would've only moved twenty yards by the time you were packing it all away again."

"Mmmm, bacon and eggs," said Harry.

"Could we not talk about fried food?" asked Amy.

"Who fancies a little game then?" said Bev.

"You mean eye-spy," said Ross, indifferently.

"I mean *any* game," said Bev.

"I spy with my big eye, something beginning with R," said Harry.

"It's my *little* eye," said Ross.

"We play by different rules," said Harry.

"Oh? Such as…?"

"Well, we play with a big eye, for one thing… and it's a pound for every incorrect answer."

"Rubbish."

"That's a pound you owe me."

"Road," said Bev.

"Yes, well done, Bev. Ross, you can give that pound to Bev."

"Can someone please put the radio on," said Ross.

Laura hit the button and Mozart filled the vehicle.

"Isn't there something else?" said Ross. "Like Radio One?"

Laura changed the station. It sounded like the singer was threatening them from the speakers.

"I preferred Beethoven," said Bev.

"It was Mozart," said Amy. "And I prefer it too."

Harry pressed a button to change the station and got a political debate.

"That doesn't sound like Beethoven," said Bev.

"Or Mozart," said Amy.

"We'll just catch up with the gist of it," said Harry.

"Why?" said Laura.

"You can't beat a bit of political rough-and-tumble," said Harry. "It's like rocket fuel for conversation."

"We are *not* having a political debate at this hour in this car," said Laura.

"Especially as the man on the radio's got it all wrong," said Bev.

Laura switched the radio off.

"Ah," said Harry, "there's the problem."

Up ahead, vehicles were being forced to change lanes to avoid a broken down Winnebago motor-home.

"At least they'll be comfortable," said Bev. "They've probably got a TV in there."

"What do you mean, comfortable?" Ross snorted. "They're blocking the road."

"It's better than breaking down in a car," Bev insisted.

"Oh good for them," said Ross. "They can sit and watch a movie while they're stopping other people using the road."

But Laura was happy. The traffic was beginning to move freely again. They'd soon be on the Lymington to Yarmouth ferry and her family would regain its spirit of harmony.

"We should be okay now," she said.

A few moments later, Ross complained.

"You're doing sixty," he said.

"I know," said Laura. "That should get us there in time."

"The speed limit's seventy. You can go faster."

"I can't. Not with four generations of this family in the car."

Ross wasn't impressed. "We're being overtaken by a thirty-year-old Renault towing a caravan."

"Uh-oh, Evie's straining," said Amy. "She might need

a change pretty soon."

"I could do with paying a visit rather urgently too," said Harry.

A moment later, a terrible aroma assaulted Laura's nostrils. Oh God, she thought. Is that the baby or Harry?

3

Somewhere Across The Sea

#13. horacewimp

Posted 15 years ago

Not sure if anyone is still following this thread but I went to Hopton's, Sandy Bay in 1976 when I was sixteen. I was stuck with my parents and twelve-year-old sister. Best holiday ever though as the weather was a million degrees and I fell deeply in love with Tammy from Cardiff. Can't recall her last name. Where are you Tammy? You must be sixty by now. Do you remember me? Bob the curly haired boy? Spoiler alert. I'm no longer curly, or indeed 'haired'.

Freddie Archer replied 15 years ago

Hi, horacewimp. Freddie here. I worked at Hopton's, Sandy Bay for two seasons, 1969 and '70, but I recall 1976. By then I was an office worker in London wishing I could be back on the Isle of Wight. That was such a long hot summer. Wonderful memories.

*

It was just after ten-thirty as they joined the slow-moving line of cars queueing for the ferry at Lymington dockside. Laura's heart was still pounding. She hated playing the racing driver, even if Ross had insisted they were in danger of being overtaken by bicycles.

It was a joy to finally be limited to a mere two miles an hour. The scene had none of the magic of that old cine footage though, when her parents' car boarded that old ferry.

Twenty minutes later, they were safely aboard the modern ferry – something of a leviathan compared with the tiny craft of 1967. The family was now free to stroll on deck, where Amy explained to Harry that the 'scruffy' pedestrians were heading for the Isle of Wight Pop Festival. Laura was relieved. With the fresh sea air in her nostrils and the thrum of the boat's engines starting up somewhere below, she let out a long sigh. They would be off soon.

"Everyone okay?" asked Harry.

"Fine, thanks," said Amy, leading a general consensus.

"How about you, Ross?" Harry asked. "Stomach okay?"

"I'm fine."

"It creeps up on you, sea-sickness."

"We haven't left the dock."

"Yes, but when we do, it could strike in minutes. Your best policy is to look at the horizon."

Laura recalled being a kid. She always looked at the horizon when they crossed the Solent. It was like going to America, not some island ten miles off the coast of southern England.

"There's a first time for everything," Harry went on. "You're a tax collector, not a round the world yachtsman."

"I'm a tax *inspector*, and I'm fine."

"What did you have for breakfast? Nothing greasy, I hope?"

"If you must know, I had cereal."

"Well, be on full alert. If you vomit on those suede shoes of yours, that's a hundred quid down the drain."

Laura wandered off and left them to it. Her mind was heading back to the past. The cars were so different then, as were the fashions people wore. She could see her parents looking young in those far off days. She could see her grandparents messing around.

And then another memory flared.

The boy.

It was silly. Nothing more than a schoolgirl fantasy. It didn't exist in her regular life, but as soon as she boarded an Isle of Wight ferry…

She's eleven years old. She's with her family in a seaside café. A boy of her age comes to take their order. She's drawn to how grown up he's attempting to be. Their eyes meet and she likes him. Then he speaks to her. "Would you like strawberry or apricot jam?"

Laura tried to shake off a sense of wistfulness. What was she lamenting? The passing of more than forty years? Had she met him just that one time, he would be long forgotten by now. But they returned when she was thirteen, fourteen, and fifteen. He became part of her Isle of Wight holiday experience, with the ferry crossing always bringing on a desire to visit the cream teas café where the boy helped out.

It also made each homeward bound ferry crossing a growing emotional challenge. At eleven and thirteen, she was sad. At fourteen, she was overcome with salty tears for her unrequited love. At fifteen, the journey home filled her with a determination to approach the boy next time and make herself known to him. However, her next visit to the island came many years later when she was married and Amy was young. They didn't even stay on the boy's side of the island and any visits to Sandy Bay were brief, without a cream tea. This time they would be staying at Hopton's holiday camp right by the village.

She laughed.

Although…

In a way, it was just an enjoyable wallow in past emotions. Where was the harm? And what burning feelings she had back then…

Thankfully, she was a cool person these days. At fifty-two, Laura Cass didn't do turbulence.

"We're off!" said Harry, as the ferry began to ease away from the dock.

They were leaving mainland England. Ten days on an island awaited them. What would it bring? A thought flashed across Laura's mind – the boy, now a nicely matured man, serving her a cream tea.

Yum.

"Mum, Bev, Harry, get in close – Ross is filming." It was Amy coming over with Evie safely strapped to her in a papoose-style baby carrier. Ross was coming along behind them, filming on his phone.

"I've put that filter on," he said. "It'll be exactly like those old home movies."

Laura smiled. It was a nice gesture. Of course, the glow of those old films was partly down to the subject matter – in that it could never be recreated by technology because youth and, in some cases, life itself, had been stolen away by time.

"Everyone feeling okay?" Harry asked.

"Yes," was the united response.

Amy smiled into Ross's phone camera. Baby Evie stayed asleep.

"Don't forget to look at the horizon, Laura," said Harry.

"I won't. Thanks for your concern."

Laura turned and felt the wind in her face. Up ahead, the island would gradually grow.

And he would come to her.

At least, in spirit.

Her heart beat a little faster, causing her to almost laugh again. This was utterly ridiculous. She was a grown woman. But she liked the feeling all the same.

"Anyone need a mint?" Harry asked. "Keep the sickness down?"

While he distributed Polos to all, Laura eyed Amy. She wanted her daughter to have the best of being a mother and a woman. Somehow, that balance had escaped Laura and her marriage to Jonathan suffered for it. This ten day break would be the longest time she'd spent with Amy in more than a decade. Whatever wasn't working, they would fix it.

Her phone pinged.

It was Angela with more ideas that Laura might want to pursue.

Laura felt like chucking her phone into the sea.

But no, she would be able to set aside a couple of mornings to keep up to date with her boss's plans. It wouldn't spoil a wonderful, relaxing holiday. In so many ways, she was indebted to Angela. Laura had been a support worker in a school that had its budget cut. Angela, a woman she'd worked with years earlier, had just started a one-woman education consultancy and came to the rescue.

Her phone pinged again.

It was Angela – again.

Could Laura squeeze in a teensy little video call next week?

Only an hour.

Two at the most.

4

Hopton's Holiday Park

#14. Alexander The Great

Posted 15 years ago

Loved the camp, loved the holidays we had there (three times). Loved the people, the orange coats, the beach, the village of Sandy Bay, the cafés, pubs, shops and the nice little hotel (which was a pub with rooms above) with the restaurant where my dad had lobster while we had fish and chips. Haven't been there since the eighties. Happy memories tho'.

*

They arrived at the camp at just after one in the afternoon. Just seeing Hopton's seashell themed signpost and rainbow of flags flooded Laura with relief and anticipation. She had successfully delivered her family to the place that would be their home for the next ten days. It was going to be brilliant.

Pulling up in the main parking area, there was a view of the sea and the hills jutting into it left and right to form the bay. The village and beach, although nearer, were tucked out of sight below the hill the camp stood on.

"Right," said Laura, "I'll see if I can get the keys."

"We're too early," said Harry. "They won't have finished cleaning the chalet."

"They might," said Laura.

"You don't know what state it's been left in by the last lot. They might have had bad toilet habits. Not everyone's like Bev, cleaning the place professionally before they leave."

"Even so," said Laura, getting out of the car, "I'll try."

Approaching the reception area in the main building, she was transported back across the years to being with her sister, Mandy. They used to get so excited.

We're going into this building and they're going to give us keys to our new home by the sea!

Mandy had taken that excitement to new levels her whole life since. No children for her and hubby Llewellyn, just an endless round of trips to places no one had heard of. Even now they were in South America exploring ancient Mayan ruins.

Laura gave her details to a young female receptionist.

"Yes, yours is ready."

"Great, thanks," said Laura.

A few minutes later, they were driving at five miles an hour to chalet 44 to drop off their gear before putting the Toyota back in the car park.

It didn't take long for Laura and her family to be safely ensconced in their white, weather-boarded cabin. With three bedrooms, a kitchen-diner-lounge, and sliding glass doors leading to a generous-size concrete patio situated to the side, they were very happy. The interior did have a strange smell, although Laura couldn't settle on what it might be. Something to do with furniture polish, heat, and a lounge carpet that had been trampled by countless sweaty, bare feet. Open windows and patio doors would soon fix it, she decided.

"Right," said Harry, "who's going to do the old holiday camp joke?"

"Pardon?" said Ross.

"It's traditional," said Harry. "Years ago, these places looked like prison camps, so whenever you met anyone, you'd say you were thinking of forming an escape committee."

"That's not funny," said Ross.

"Of course it isn't," said Harry, "but back in the days before people plugged themselves into a smart phone, we had something called conversation. You'd meet a stranger staying next door on the camp, use an icebreaker like the escape committee joke, and you'd begin a friendly relationship that would last the rest of the holiday."

Ross shrugged and checked his phone.

"You see that building over there," said Bev, pointing through the open patio doors, unperturbed. "That's where they had the ballroom."

Laura was studying a pamphlet showing a map of the camp.

"According to this, it still is."

"I mean the original ballroom. The one with all the memories."

"Yeah," said Harry. "The new one's bound to smell of plastic. And we'll be overcharged at the bar and surrounded by people taking selfies. *And* we won't have a proper comedian."

Laura took the baby from Amy, who looked hopelessly tired.

"Thanks Mum. Would you mind if get an hour's sleep?"

"Of course not. You go ahead."

"I think I'll scope out the camp store later," said Ross. "See if they've heard of vaping."

"Just think," said Bev as Amy left them, "this family's getaways go back a hundred years."

Laura knew the story of how her great-grandfather had been a successful businessman who took the family to Eastbourne on the Sussex coast every year – until he went bust.

"I wonder if they still run a Glamourous Granny competition?" said Harry, studying the camp's schedule.

"Ooh, I could have a go," said Bev.

"You're not a gran," said Harry. "You're a great-gran."

"I'm a gran to Amy."

"Isn't that a purely ceremonial role now?" questioned Harry.

"Don't be ridiculous," said Laura.

"I'm only joking," said Harry. "We're not *that* old."

"Exactly," said Bev.

"No," said Harry. "We'll know when we're *really* old. That's when the family only shows up for our birthdays and funerals."

Laura stepped outside with Evie to take the air.

"You see that, Evie? It's changed a bit from my days."

It was still possible to see it as it had once been. And that brought distant echoes of games and laughter. For a moment, she could picture her grandparents, Joan and Stan, throwing a beach ball to each other over the upward reaching arms of little Laura and her older sister Mandy, leaping as high as they could to catch a ball against a dazzling blue sky.

"Do you want tomato in your sandwich, Laura?" Bev asked from the patio doorway.

"Yes, please."

"A penny for them?" Bev added.

Laura shrugged. "Oh... just thinking of times past. Gran and Grandad, really."

Bev smiled. Joan and Stan were her much loved, much missed parents.

"The good ol' days, eh?" she said before disappearing back inside.

Harry replaced Bev in the doorway, and then stepped onto the patio.

"Talking about the old days, eh?"

"Oh, not really, Harry. Just a memory."

Ross came outside.

"So were the old holiday camps really terrible?"

"No," said Harry. "It's what people were used to. The main thing was the affordable price. See, Billy Butlin insisted families should be able to enjoy a holiday at one of his camps for the equivalent of a week's pay. Their slogan was 'Our True Intent Is All For Your Delight'."

"That's a bit clunky," said Ross. "It wouldn't get the nod at a modern branding agency."

"Millions of people went to Butlin's, Pontin's, Warner's, Hopton's," said Harry, "all making wonderful memories simply because their families were spending time together away from home, school and work."

"I remember the activities," said Laura. "Funfair rides, the boating lake, talent contests, beauty pageants, knobbly knees..." She peered at Evie. "You've got knobbly knees, haven't you."

"Not many of the family camps have survived," said Harry. "These companies operate spa hotels now, or if it's a camp, it'll be adults only."

"This place seems stuck in the past," said Ross, looking around.

"There's nothing wrong with the past," said Harry.

"I also remember the Punch & Judy shows down by

the beach," said Laura. "And the donkey rides."

"We're not missing much there," said Ross.

"You have to take it in context," said Harry. "Years ago, summer meant a mass migration from the factories and offices. Whole towns would shut down for the same two weeks. It was a chance to board a steam train or a bus down to the coast. A week or two away from the grime and drudgery. From Brighton to Blackpool, Skegness to… somewhere beginning with S…"

"Sidmouth?" Laura suggested.

"That'll have to do. Anyway, it was a golden age, Ross. Crowds of people descending on the grand hotels, holiday camps and seaside landladies. You had the big ballrooms, the piers, the theatres offering big names to make you laugh or sing. And then you had fish and chips on the promenade. That's why everyone wrote the same thing on their postcards back home – 'wish you were here.' It was a different world."

"I suppose," said Ross.

"It still applies today," said Harry. "It's a holiday, a break, a vacation, an escape. For ten days we'll live a completely different way of life. Use it well."

Laura took Evie onto the communal green, bouncing her granddaughter gently against her shoulder. A mum, dad and a young boy were watching her from the patio of Chalet 43 situated about thirty feet away. They had also just arrived. The boy, who looked about five, was holding a yellow and blue striped football.

"He should be in school," the father explained, "but it's the only time we can afford a proper two-week break. They double the prices during the summer holidays."

"No need to explain," said Laura.

"We got a fifty quid fine," he went on, "but we saved three hundred. Are you the same as us – a Friday to

Friday fortnight?"

"No… ten days, Friday to Monday week."

"We don't agree with kids missing school," said the mother, "but we think it's important they have a family holiday."

"Absolutely," said Laura.

"They do Saturday to Saturday, too," said the father. "It's very flexible."

"Yes, and Monday to Monday," said Laura, now at the limit of her interest in the matter.

"Perhaps we'll go into the village after lunch," Bev called from inside number 44.

Laura quite fancied that. It was time she got reacquainted with the streets, shops, and cafés down by the beach.

5

The Village

I loved holidays with my mum and dad at Hopton's in Sandy Bay! Dad was a steel worker, always grubby and worried about work and stuff. Then for 2 weeks he was my real dad, carefree, laughing, smiling, playing games with me. Mum and me miss him so much. We're just glad we have all the photos from those far-off summer days. Such happy faces. Such wonderful times.

*

After a light lunch and an hour of general dozing, the family prepared to move out. Standing outside chalet 44, Laura looked out to sea. Soon, they would descend the hill and find what awaited them tucked below and out of view for now.

"All set?" Bev asked.

All confirmed they were. Even Evie was wide awake in her buggy.

"A journey of a thousand miles starts with a single

step," said Harry. "And I should know. I had a car like that. At the start of every journey, you'd have to get out and push."

With a collective groan, they headed off down a path between the next few chalets, across an internal road, past all the main buildings and pool, and then down through the caravan side of the park. Finally, they reached the rear gate – a four-foot break in the dry stone wall – that led to the road in and out of the village.

Upward to the right, the road rose along with a parallel footpath to the top of the hill overlooking the bay from the east side. Downward, to the left, it led to the seafront, beach, and Sandy Bay's Fore Street.

Walking down the road to the village at three p.m., the heat of the day had yet to diminish. Indeed the sun, although supposedly beginning its descent, continued to dazzle from high up – especially where it reflected off the occasional white-painted building.

A delivery truck chugged by, on its way out. Laura felt the drone of its engine vibrating in the air.

At the bottom of the road, the whole vista widened, with the busy beach just ahead. She loved the gentle waves hitting the shoreline and the squeals of children splashing and playing with beach balls and sandcastles. And then there were the reds, yellows, blues and greens of the umbrellas, deck chairs, and sun loungers. Holidaymakers, young and old. The smell of sea and sunscreen, and of vinegar on fish and chips. Under the glorious summer sun, it looked so full of promise.

"It's lovely," said Amy.

"It is," said Laura.

Last time they came to the Isle of Wight, they stayed elsewhere and only came this way for a brief look. Since then, Amy had been away to university for three years, and then lived in Manchester for another three. She returned to London at the same time as Laura began working for Angela, so it had been difficult to find the time to team up. This holiday, thankfully, would put that right.

They moved on, heading left where the road joined Fore Street, the village's main avenue. Laura knew that halfway along this byway of local shops, Bay Street would branch off to the left for fifty yards before stopping at the Island pub and beer garden. And a certain café.

She loved the whole scene, with people moving slowly from one shop to the next. This was the way to relax. Ten days of loafing around. Obviously, with a few hours dedicated to Angela's requests, but still tons of Laura Time and Family Time. It was perfect.

As they strolled, she tried to recall more details. She had visited the Isle of Wight aged six months, two years, five, eleven, thirteen, fourteen, fifteen, twenty-six, thirty-one, forty-two, and now fifty-two – but it was a journey into a half-remembered world. Things changed year on year and it had been a long time since her last visit. Even now, she was wondering…

Wasn't there a baker's over there…? Isn't that the restaurant that did good food…? Doesn't the end of Fore Street lead to a jetty…?

She glanced down an alley to get a glimpse behind the scenes – yes, stacks of bagged waste and folded cardboard. This was a place of commerce, no doubt about that.

"It's gone!" Bev gasped.

"What's gone?" said Harry.

"That little place there. I used to buy a seaside thimble every time I came here."

"The Aztec Restaurant," said Harry, reading the sign.

"You could buy a burrito and put it on display in the French cabinet at home."

"That's not funny, Harry. I know things have to change, but it's a shame when it's a knick-knack shop. I used to spend hours looking around in there."

"I'm sure there are other knick-knack shops," said Laura.

Bev's displeasure faded and they walked on for a bit, enjoying the ambience of the sun baked street full of happy visitors.

It wasn't long before they reached the corner of Fore and Bay Streets where Laura's imagination flared a little.

"Anyone fancy a cream tea?" said Bev. "If I remember rightly, there's a place just up here."

The consensus was all for it, leading Laura to consider the most ridiculous possibility in summer holiday history.

Would *he* be there?

That first fantasy, at eleven, had been one of a simple friendship becoming marriage and happiness. It was all very innocent. Naturally, the hormonal teen fantasies contained a little more heat, but were just as unrealistic. Time, however, had imbued these fantasies with a power – and, at a busy time in her real life, didn't their innocent perfection offer something of an escape?

She dismissed it as utter nonsense and followed the others into Bay Street. It wasn't as if the boy from the café had been truly special. Didn't she almost have a fling with another boy, one from Liverpool, when she was fifteen? So why this boy? She trod the fantasy down. It was a summer's day, she was on holiday, and the desire to sit outside a café eating cream scones was overwhelming.

"Actually, we haven't long had lunch," Ross complained. "Maybe we should skip the cream teas. I was thinking of having a 5k run later."

They came to a halt with Harry tutting.

"Here's an idea," said Laura, "how about Ross has a green tea and the rest of us stuff our faces?"

There was a swift agreement and they continued on their way to the café. Laura was pleased. For ten days only, she would at last have some control over her life.

They soon arrived at the place Laura knew as the Bayside Café, only it had been renamed The Complete Treat. She wondered. Would it still have the courtyard out the back? The one that adjoined an open green space and, a little farther on, the Island pub's beer garden?

They went inside. The counter was different. In fact, everything was different. It was definitely the place, but… when she was eleven, there were framed pictures on the walls. Pastel shades with small boats bobbing by a pier, a lighthouse, a seagull over a beach. By the time she was fifteen, the décor had switched to physical art: a ship's wheel, a fisherman's netting, a lifebelt. Now the walls were home to large posters proclaiming the joys of local attractions such as Osborne House, The Needles, and Carisbrooke Castle.

A man came out to help the woman at the counter. He was around Laura's age. Was this him? The boy? Was it that simple? Did you just return after forever and find him there, waiting?

It seemed utterly ridiculous.

Of course, it was hard to discern the boy's face behind an older face augmented with glasses and a silver beard. The lack of hair didn't help much either. Still, she supposed the people who lived and worked in places such as this often had a lifelong connection. It didn't seem likely that new people would come in every few years.

"Hello," he said. "What can I get you?"

The voice? It was the exact same accent, although she

still couldn't be certain.

Harry stepped in. "Tea and cream scones with strawberry jam for four, please. What about you, Ross?"

"Actually, I'll have a cream tea too, please."

Bev insisted on paying and then they passed through the café into a half full rear courtyard that did indeed adjoin the green and pub beer garden much as Laura had remembered it. With its wrought iron tables and mish-mash of chairs; some iron with floral seat cushions and others of green plastic, it really did look the same, but somehow it felt utterly different.

Stepping out onto the green, she gazed at the estuary that fed into the bay, where the small boats moored at a number of jetties. All looked still. Beyond the boats, the hills rose up, one of which jutted out to sea to form the western boundary of the bay.

"This hasn't changed much," she said as she rejoined her family, who had taken their seats.

"I hope I haven't made a faux pas," said Harry. "I should have checked no-one's allergic to strawberry jam. Imagine if Ross's body couldn't handle strawberries."

"It can," Ross assured him.

"No, but you read about these things, don't you. A seemingly fit and healthy young man eats strawberry jam, falls off his chair and is rushed to hospital with his face resembling a giant strawberry."

"I'll be fine," said Ross.

"I didn't know people could be allergic to strawberries," said Bev.

"People can be allergic to anything," said Harry. "I once read about a woman who was allergic to eating bananas near oak trees."

"Rubbish," said Ross.

"That does sound unlikely," said Amy.

"Unlikely, but true. She will die if she eats a banana while standing near an oak tree. It's a chemical combination. Basically, her head will swell to twice its size and kill her."

"How did she find out she had this condition?" Ross asked.

"Obviously, she only ate part of the banana and was, maybe, standing a little farther away from the tree, meaning her head only inflated slightly."

"Ridiculous," said Ross.

"Well, I'll keep an eye on you while you eat your scone," Harry assured him. "Just to make sure your head doesn't get any bigger."

The talk at their table switched to the coming days. What would they do? Where would they go? Who liked steam railways? Who wanted to see the model village? Could you enjoy a seaside holiday without going on a pier?

And Laura joined in ninety percent.

It wasn't the fantasy itself, she decided. It was the absence of a relationship in her life that gave oxygen to such daft thoughts. Somehow, her subconscious mind was doing its bit to nudge her into getting a partner. If that meant some Disney-esque Cinderella reboot, then she just needed to understand that's all it was. She was free to let it slide past – although there was no harm in enjoying the silliness of it in private for a while.

The man who might have been the boy, accompanied by the woman from the counter, brought their cream teas on two trays. As the accoutrements were set out for them, Laura considered asking if he might be the boy. She could feel the question rising up from her chest. In the heat of the moment, it felt too stupid and too pitiful. Thankfully, Harry cut across her.

"Do you have many people collapse with swollen heads?"

Both servers seemed to struggle with any kind of answer.

"Of course they don't," said Bev. "This is strawberry, not banana, and there isn't an oak tree in sight."

"Enjoy," said the man who might have been the boy.

Laura tucked into her scone. The thick cream wouldn't kill many people in terms of allergies, but Ross was right about its power to take down a few by clogging their arteries. Although… the delicious taste was far too good to worry about any potential health fallout.

And as for the boy…

He was probably married with grown up children. No, it was a silly, fun fantasy but time had moved on. She was a logical, sensible person who created tailored training days for education professionals. So, no, she wouldn't be asking the man if he'd been the boy. The boy had disappeared. Gone. Never to be seen again.

She was used to that. Her dad had been and gone. Her ex too. Not death, but walking out on twenty years of marriage. But Laura was okay. Jonathan had left and that was in the past. Besides, Angela had made her feel good again by placing trust in her abilities. At fifty-two, she didn't require candle-lit dinners to be happy. Her ideal treat was a solo trip to an out-of-town historic building with lunch and a stroll in which she could reflect on life in some far off period – the people, their hopes, their fears, their deeds and misdeeds. She felt it was a good use of her free time. Not boring at all.

She'd read a book about that – how to avoid being boring.

"You alright?" Harry asked

"Absolutely," Laura assured him.

Harry turned to Ross.

"No reaction to the jam?"

"I'm fine."

"You look a bit red in the face."

"I said I'm fine."

"Airways clear?"

"Perfectly clear, thank you."

In her mind, Laura asked the man if he'd been the boy and he said yes. They followed this up by going for a drink and getting to know each other. It was all looking very promising. In reality, she smothered another piece of scone with cream and strawberry jam and took a bite. The main thing was enjoying ten whole days away from the hurly-burly of her everyday life in London. A chance to relax and unwind. An opportunity to recharge the batteries before she returned to work. And, for ten days, she was in control. That much felt very good indeed.

6

The One That Got Away...?

#16: Freddie Archer

Posted 14 years ago

Hello everyone. It's Freddie here again. I see no one has written a comment recently. Will the tourism people keep this part of the website open indefinitely? As I've said previously, I went to Hopton's, Sandy Bay as a twelve-year-old boy. I loved it so much I got a job there ten years later and stayed for a couple of seasons. I actually fell in love with an orange coat without her knowledge (shy young man syndrome!) but she left to work somewhere in London (as did I, working in insurance, although our paths never crossed again). My wife died three years ago and my daughter works in America. Sandy Bay is a truly special place. I'll go back again one day.

> Realdealdave replied 14 years ago
>
> We've been regulars at Hopton's Sandy Bay for 15 years. Last time was last July. It's gradually declined over the years though, and

will be closing for good in September. Very sad.

Freddie Archer replied 14 years ago

Thanks for replying. I didn't know that. As you say, very sad.

*

"Do you remember the exact day we met?" Jonathan asked.

"Yes, I remember," Laura murmured. It was good to be in each other's arms. "I arrived on the Friday and met you on the Saturday – thereby confirming that Saturday is always the best day of the week."

She recalled the fierce heat of that holiday in Portugal and the fact that everyone was wearing as little as possible, especially when messing around by the pool. Just like her, he was there with friends. They were all in their early twenties and she got the idea his mates were only in Portugal for one thing. Okay, maybe three things if you included sunshine and beer.

She and Jonathan hit it off and seemed to have something more than the physical side of things – which they enjoyed as much as anyone. But when it turned out they lived a mere five miles apart across the north-east London suburbs, they decided – against their friends' advice – to meet up when they got back home.

They were married a year later.

Jonathan kissed her neck, which she liked, but he seemed to become lighter and actually began to float away. She had to hold on to him…

She opened her eyes in a strange room, alone in bed.

Fifteen minutes later, she had showered and dressed and was first to the breakfast table. It was 6:45 on Saturday morning and she had never felt so un-relaxed. Did she actually have an off-switch?

Munching on toast and sipping coffee, she flicked through Facebook. There was a post from her old school page. She never posted anything herself, but she enjoyed reading the comments of her former contemporaries. She'd hear their voices, too – at least their teenage voices, having no idea what they sounded like in their fifties. The latest post related to last night's TV, which she hadn't seen.

Jonathan once said their lives were moving at different speeds. That probably explained how he'd practically moved out before she realized there was a problem. He very patiently explained that when one partner is developing while the other is inactive, it can cause relational divergence.

Of course, Laura immediately swung into action. She suggested doing lots of things together, like having weekends away to visit historic buildings, but Jonathan said his long, unpredictable work hours in television production prevented him from committing to a planned lifestyle.

She went to the marriage guidance people, where a very young woman suggested rekindling things in a more imaginative hands-on fashion. But Jonathan said he couldn't respond to a woman who had swallowed a 'how to' book rather than one who was genuinely hungry for him. He said there was no blame but two decades of motherhood had established her priorities and he didn't want to be brought back into her emotional life solely because Amy had gone away to university.

She did seek further advice, but Jonathan cut it short by announcing he'd met a woman called Catherine who had reinvigorated him, no doubt in a more imaginative hands-on fashion. For a few years after, Laura couldn't face romantic movies and novels because she could only see her ex and Catherine in the roles of those overcoming various obstacles to fall into each other's arms and live happily ever after. Movies and books didn't spend much time highlighting the plight of the wife who had been pigeonholed as boring. At that time, she didn't feel boring. She just felt lost.

Her phone pinged.

It was an email from Angela.

Laura lamented the time her internet service provider had taken to deliver something obviously sent last night – but then double checked the time stamp. Angela had just sent it.

Laura sighed. What was her boss doing up at this hour?

> Hi Laura
> How about this for the new website.
>
> "In order to make your training session the best it can be, please complete our pre-booking questionnaire. By knowing your objectives, we'll make sure the course is right for you. If we or you feel the course needs changes to better suit your needs, we'll do that at no extra cost. Only when you're entirely happy will a booking fee become payable."
>
> Laura, could you create a questionnaire and show some examples of how a couple of standard courses might be tweaked in the light of different

answers given in the questionnaire.
Many thanks
A.

Laura checked her weather app. It was going to be hotter than yesterday. Whichever measure you preferred, 82° F or 28° C, the sun screen would be seeing plenty of action.

She went back to her room and lay on top of the duvet in her clothes.

An hour passed without sleep.

As she returned to the lounge area, Bev emerged from her room heading for the loo.

"You're up early, Laura."

"Couldn't sleep. Do you and Harry want tea yet?"

"Give it a bit longer, love. We're on holiday."

"Yes, of course."

We're on holiday…

Before Bev had closed the bathroom door, Laura made up her mind about something.

"I'm going for a walk, Mum. I'll see you later."

"Okay, love, have fun."

"I will."

*

In the relatively cool morning air, Laura headed out through the camp's back gate and down the road into the village. The sun was climbing higher in the blue and glinting in silvery flashes off the water. It was picture postcard perfect, but she pushed on with barely a glance, past the beach, and into Fore Street with thoughts swooping like seagulls.

I never have fun anymore. Actual silly fun.

Everything's serious. If I don't deliver a good training session, the nation's teachers will fail, our schools will fail and Britain will no doubt sink into a morass and turn communist.

She turned left into Bay Street. It didn't take long to reach the end.

Naturally, the Complete Treat did a different selection of goodies first thing in the morning. Right now, not long after eight o'clock, the door was open to the public and the air was rich with the aromas of fresh coffee and fried bacon.

She felt like a spy.

Mission: evaluate target for possible wild holiday romance.

Engage special equipment.

Er… eyes, ears.

Does he shower?

Engage nose.

Nose failure due to coffee and bacon overload.

The target was serving a young man, possibly the driver of the electrician's van parked outside. A couple of middle-aged women were having coffee at a table. A young woman dodged past Laura to get inside. Then the man who might have been the boy glanced over and saw her.

Abort, abort.

She hadn't planned what to say.

Laura walked on, into the Island pub's empty beer garden. From there she gazed across the parched green, beyond the café's outdoor tables, to the estuary and the hills beyond. What would the man who had been the boy make of her? Would he think her a fool? Or would she think she was throwing herself at him with a cheesy chat up line? Maybe he took advantage of divorced, middle-aged women who came to Sandy Bay. Or maybe he wouldn't think any of that at all. Maybe he was just a nice guy who happened to work at the seaside. Maybe he was already in a relationship. Maybe he had a wife and children.

Laura went back to the café and paused outside. She supposed she'd known him all her life. So, no, it would just be a simple catch-up.

The mission is back on.

Move in.

Go, go, go.

"A cappuccino, please," she said as she approached the counter.

She was soon at a table in the corner, sipping her coffee and checking Facebook. She felt the heat rising. She hadn't experienced a racing heart in many a year. How would this play out? What did she even want from him?

She thought back to meeting Jonathan on holiday. That had been perfectly normal. And how did that end? She thought of the boy. What if he was the one that got away? Was meeting him now any different from meeting Jonathan all those years ago? Who got to decide what was normal and what was crazy?

No, this was definitely crazy. Not right at all. She wanted to feel again, but this was all wrong.

She finished her coffee and left.

Making her way onto the dry green, she gazed upon the small boats in the estuary. Chatting with the man about those far off days would simply be nice. It wouldn't be weird at all. If anything came of it, fine. If not, that would also be fine.

So what was the problem?

The destruction of a harmless forty-years-long fantasy created by an eleven-year-old girl. That was the problem.

Meeting the man who had been the boy would be a kind of death.

All the same, she walked back to the café and approached the man behind the counter.

"I wonder if you could help me," she asked.

7

Life's A Beach

#17: John Smith 1898

Posted 14 years ago

I remember going to Hopton's in the early 60s when me and my brother were kids. I think our parents might have been there with us but we were out cycling, swimming and exploring all day, every day, so I can't be 100% sure. One day, we cycled five miles from the camp before we decided it was time to turn back. We were 9 and 7 at the time. Honestly, though, it was a great rest for Mum and Dad, who worked hard all year.

*

Laura returned from her walk to find the rest of the family on the patio enjoying coffee. Evie had joined them in her high chair and was busy gnawing on a messy rusk.

"How about we go out?" said Ross. "We could search the other side of the island."

"What for?" said Harry. "We're on *this* side of the island. Why travel to where we're not just to search?"

"It does seem an extra effort," said Bev.

"That's not how Columbus discovered America, Bev," said Ross.

"He had a ship," said Harry. "We've got a car. Not even a proper car. It's more like a van. Anyway, the other side of the island's been discovered."

"There are a couple of tourist attractions we'll be visiting over the other side of the island," said Laura. "I'm sure we can add in a little look around while we're there."

"If we're just nosing around, there must be places we can go locally," said Amy. "As long as it's safe for Evie."

"I agree with Amy," said Harry.

"Well, I'd like to do something fun," said Ross. "I don't mind what – scuba diving, water-skiing, rock climbing, paragliding…"

Laura knew that Ross had become a regular at the gym and that he looked up to the more experienced guys there. She hoped he hadn't come to the Isle of Wight just to get photos that would impress them.

"Rock climbing, paragliding…" Harry mulled. "Is this a face your fears thing, Ross? You can do that by getting rid of the spider by the fridge. Amy says you're scared of them."

"No, I'm not…"

But Ross's response was cut short by a loud cheer. A crocodile line of thirty or so children led by half a dozen orange coats was coming along the main path. They came to a halt by Chalet 43, where the young boy was on the patio with his parents. The boy was entreated to join the line for a gold coin hunt. He did so without hesitation, which raised another loud cheer. Then off they went, looking for more participants.

"You don't get that in a hotel," said Harry.

Laura watched the parents go inside and close the patio doors. Harry was watching too.

"I bet they're not locking themselves in to do a word puzzle," he said.

"Don't be so nosy," said Bev.

"I'm just saying it's a great service for parents," said Harry. "A bit like Sunday School was when I was young."

"We don't need to hear all that," said Bev.

Laura envied the couple in Chalet 43. She quite fancied being in love with a guy and having a free hour or so.

She thought back to her chat with the man who used to be the boy.

Clive.

She'd enquired about the family who ran the place in the late seventies, early eighties and they had a lovely, if brief chat about the old days. And, what's more, he recalled her coming in all those years ago.

She said she'd see him again at two, when he'd take his break and have a bit more time for a proper catch-up. She still wasn't completely and absolutely certain how she felt about that, but it undoubtedly offered a chance for something interesting to shake up the void in her personal life.

"How about a swim in the sea?" said Ross. "We could work up an appetite."

"Oh, I don't know," said Harry. "I haven't swum in the sea since that movie."

Laura's brow furrowed. "What movie?" She hoped he wasn't going to say Jaws.

"Jaws," said Harry.

Ross scoffed. "Jaws was back in the seventies."

"It just goes to show how good it was then," said Harry. "I haven't been in the sea since."

"That's silly," said Ross.

"There's no chance of a great white shark getting its teeth into me," Harry insisted.

"There are no great whites off the English coast," said Ross.

"How do you know? I mean there's you, all confident, getting in the water, and the next thing we see is your leg being washed up."

"That's ridiculous."

"That's what happened to that girl."

"What girl?" Amy asked.

"The girl in Jaws," said Harry.

"Well, I'll risk it," said Ross.

"Fine," said Harry. "Just try to avoid the jellyfish. One sting from a Portuguese Man of War and your arms will swell up making it impossible to swim."

"Put some sunscreen on," said Bev.

"Don't worry, I will," said Ross, "along with the shark and octopus repellant."

"We'll watch from the beach," said Bev.

"Great," said Ross. "Just remember to bring a bag to collect my limbs in."

Laura went inside to get her laptop. "I've just got a bit of work to do," she reported.

"Blimey," said Harry. "In my day, when you left the office to go on holiday that was that. Nowadays, the office comes with you. Still, we mustn't hold back progress."

"No indeed," said Laura.

She wanted to tell Harry to mind his own business, but she couldn't. Now that she was finally away from the hustle and bustle for an extended period, she had a growing dread that she wouldn't be able to relax, that her brain was too fried, that the holiday would be pointless in terms of recharging her batteries, and that she'd return to work the same multi-tasking zombie she'd been before she went away.

*

It was just after ten and Laura was on the patio waiting for everyone to sort themselves out for their stroll to the beach. While there, she was watching the people in Chalet 45 packing their gear into their car. Obviously, it had been a Saturday to Saturday booking and now, in their final minutes at Sandy Bay, they looked resigned to the appalling fate of having to return home. Laura hoped they'd had fun while it lasted and had made some memories.

"Right, I'm as ready as I'll ever be," said Amy, loaded down with bags. "Baby changing stuff, baby sunscreen, baby hat, baby snacks and water, baby powder, baby blanket, baby toys... I don't think I've forgotten anything."

Ross came out holding his phone and sunglasses.

Laura's blood began to boil, but he turned to Amy and casually asked if she needed him to carry anything. Laura simmered down again.

"Did I ever tell anyone about some of the insect bites I've had?" said Harry.

He did so, in detail, all the way down to the point where the downward road reached the seafront. There, Laura embraced the scene of umbrellas, sunhats, beach balls and people stretched out on sun loungers and towels... and the waves breaking, children yelping and yelling, and radios providing pop music here and classical music there. While the sun blazed and the temperature climbed ever higher, the slight, cooling breeze off the sea made this a popular destination.

Descending the three steps from the promenade to the beach itself, the family sought a viable spot. Fortunately, it didn't take too long to find one under a large 'for hire' umbrella.

Amy duly set down her bags and got Evie comfortable for the session. Laura helped and double-checked that Evie would remain in the shade when the sun moved. Then, feeling the effects of rising so early, she smothered her exposed arms, legs and face in sunscreen and got comfortable on a towel. With her eyes soon closed, Clive came to her. They were in the back of his place. It was deserted. It was crazy, because it didn't seem right, but she wanted to feel again...

Harry's voice drifted through her thoughts.

"That's what the seaside was in Victorian times – health resorts. Suddenly, everyone thought it was a good idea to swim in the sea. Once somebody worked out you needed to entertain people after they'd come out of the water, you had your seaside resort... and a good location for a dirty weekend..."

Harry's lecture faded and Clive returned. Laura had a weird feeling they were about to get too close. And that she wanted it to happen.

*

Laura stirred. Everything seemed so bright. She was on the beach. No need to open her eyes. There were children's voices and the gentle rumble of waves breaking on the shore. It sounded perfect.

"Why don't you learn to Skype, Gran?" said Amy.

"What for?"

"To be in touch. Ross's aunt Skypes her daughter in New Zealand."

"I don't have a daughter in New Zealand."

"No, but..."

"Laura's in London, and Mandy… she's not one for making calls."

Laura hauled herself up.

"Cold drinks or ice cream, anyone?" she asked.

"What time's lunch?" said Harry.

"One o'clock back at the chalet," said Bev. "Then we'll come back to the beach at half-two till five. Then back to the chalet to rest. Then out to dinner at half-six. And then, if anyone wants to go to the ballroom, that's open till midnight."

"I'll have a ninety-nine," said Harry.

Laura took everyone's orders and went to join the line at the ice-cream shack on the promenade at the back of the beach. In front of her was the family from Chalet 43. Their five-year-old son had new water wings, a snorkel and mask, and an inflated dinosaur. They all seemed to be wearing new beachwear, sandals and sunglasses too. The father, possibly realizing he was in front of the woman from Chalet 44, gave an exaggerated shrug.

"You save a few hundred on the holiday, but spend it anyway," he said. "No real way to save money, is there." He laughed and Laura laughed a little too.

A moment later, reaching the front of the queue, she noticed the wall clock inside the shack. It was 11:30.

Only two and a half hours to go.

8

An Ocean of Love

#18: suefrombrixtonhill

Posted 13 years ago

I abso-bloody-lutely LOVED Sandy Bay. In 1976, I was at Hopton's with my sister, mum, dad, nan and grandad. Mum and Dad won a ballroom dancing competition and I came third in a fancy dress competition (I was a cardboard dinosaur). My sis and me spent a lot of time at the junior disco drinking lemonade and trying to look grown up. I was actually going to book a holiday there with my hubby and two kids but I found it's closed. What a shame. That's how I found this thread, btw.

Trevorrossington replied 13 years ago

I loved Hopton's on the Isle of Wight. Went for 10 years (age 6 to 16). Many years later, I was there the week before it closed. So many sad people. We had a brilliant time, but staff were facing redundancy. True professionals to the end, of course. Happy days, sad days. Just like life, I suppose.

*

In the Island pub's busy beer garden, Laura looked into Clive's face, trying to get a better sense of him. He was busy demolishing a cheeseburger and a beer.

"I still can't believe you remember me from all that time ago," he said between mouthfuls.

"It's like I said. I'm not crazy, but I used to have this fantasy…"

"It's not crazy. It's nice."

"It's just that I'd forget all about you when I got home. No offence."

"None taken."

"Then… next time around, I'd be boarding the ferry and guess who'd turn up on the breeze."

"Me. At least, a younger, fitter me. With hair."

"We all get older."

"What was the fantasy version of me like? Just so I know how far I fall short?"

"Oh… not fully formed really. More a presence, an essence of a man. A good man. Strong. Fair minded."

She held back on sexy.

"Hmm," he said.

"Do you know," she said, "I'm not sure this is working. I feel I've invaded your life. Please tell me you agree. I promise I won't bother you again."

He placed a hand over hers.

"It's the nicest thing that's happened in years."

She felt the warmth of his touch, of his skin against hers. This is what she'd missed these past seven years without Jonathan, and frankly, at least another seven before that.

"Let's go back," he said. "I've got some old photos to

show you."

They were soon in a room above the Complete Treat. Laura was looking at a number of photos of Sandy Bay as it was in the 1950s. They seemed to have been printed from an internet site.

"Are there any of you?" she asked.

"Hundreds," he said, "but they're all at my dad's place inland. I'll show you sometime. You'll like them."

Laura felt all wrong. Clive's room wasn't quite what she'd expected. It had been tidied but it seemed scruffy and uncared for at heart. As if someone had recently run around attempting to make it neat for a visitor.

Clive pushed the window open but no breeze came in. The outside air was too hot and still for that. The room remained stifling. Air-con was probably asking too much, but a fan?

As if reading her mind, he switched on a fan – a four-inch one taped to the shelf beside the bed.

Still, he was a reader of books. That was a good sign.

She checked the spines.

Stephen King.

Uh-oh…

Laura chastised herself. She was being too judgmental. This nice man was the boy from the past and he spent the entire summer working hard to serve holidaymakers. He probably didn't get much time to sort out his room. He probably never did much more than crash into bed at the end of a long day and haul himself out again far too early the next morning. He was obviously alone, and she guessed quite a lonely man. The boy was a source of strength to her. A force for good. A torch in the dark. The fact that Clive came out of all that promise, all that goodness… it bought him a lot of credit.

She turned to ask him something, but his lips were on

hers before she could utter a word.

Well, what did she expect? Hadn't she come here to form a bond with the boy who was now the man? And what better way to do that than enjoy his lips on hers… and his hand trying to get into her panties?

Wow, not many people get to live out their fantasy. Lucky me.

"Shall we make ourselves more comfortable," she said, pulling away.

"Yes, of course."

He sat down heavily on the bed and patted the duvet beside him. Laura worried she'd cough at the dust now visible in the air, but reminded herself that she was there because there was a great big gap in her life.

All the same, while she was forcing herself to think 'I've hit the jackpot', the rest of her brain was yelling 'get out!'

Perhaps it was the seediness of the room. Perhaps the seediness was so long-established, it had developed a personality.

"Shall we…?" Clive said.

Laura gulped.

"Water…"

"Oh, there's a tap in the bathroom."

"Ice cold water. I'm too hot."

"Downstairs," he said. "Take one from the fridge in the café. No need to pay."

Great, that's saved me a whole pound.

She hurried down the stairs and took the water from the cold drinks cabinet.

"Did you have any luck earlier?" a middle-aged woman asked. She was eating a sandwich at a table.

"Pardon?"

"Sorry to be nosy. I was in earlier and heard you asking about the original owners."

"Oh… right. I'm thinking now it might have been a mistake."

"It's a small village," said the woman. "I've lived and worked here all my life. I knew the family who ran this place in the late seventies, early eighties. They moved away years ago. There was a death in the family not that long ago. The old man. Very sad."

"They moved away?"

"Yes."

Then who the hell's trying to give me a Complete Treat?

"Clive took over about five years ago," the woman said.

Laura left the café and stood angrily outside on Bay Street. She was furious with herself. And with Clive. And with fate for taking hold of her fantasy, turning it toxic, and attempting to crush it into oblivion while destroying her self-esteem in the process. It was just a harmless fantasy. It didn't deserve that.

But then a wave of relief washed over her. Clive wasn't the man who was once the boy. He was just a bog-standard primordial opportunist creep.

"Tracy might be able to help," the woman said at the doorway. "She used to know the old owners. She runs a café at the estuary end of Fore Street. The Moorings."

"Tracy?"

"Yes, just say Janie sent you."

"Right, thanks."

Laura stormed off. She hated liars. They deserved a special kind of hell. Of course, she had no intention of calling on Tracy at the Moorings. What would be the point? Her fantasy would recover in time. The boy, whoever he'd been, would once again become the not-quite-fully-formed man. And, for ninety-nine percent of her life, she wouldn't even think about him.

*

A much calmer Laura was at the beach with her family, sitting on a towel and staring out to sea at nothing in particular. It was 2:45 and the rest of Saturday afternoon seemed to offer little other than the delicious opportunity to be lazy. On the downside, it also promised an abundance of time to mull over the Clive disaster.

"Do you know what I'm looking forward to?" said Bev, offering butter-mints to all from a pack. "Osborne House."

"Me too," said Laura, taking a couple. "Osborne House is exactly what we need."

She'd already booked the tickets for a visit to Queen Victoria's former home. Yes, focusing on the family holiday. That was the way forward. Family time. Family involvement.

Get involved.

She noticed Ross searching his phone for something. With his ear pods in, Laura guessed it was music.

"What's your beach music, Ross?"

"Uh?"

She raised her voice. "Your beach music?"

He removed a pod. "It's relaxation soundtracks. They last an hour and help you relax."

"Oh, interesting. Maybe I should try that. What kind of soundtracks are they?"

"This one's the sound of the sea."

Laura was taken aback. "The what?"

"The sound of waves breaking on the shore."

Harry was in fast. "Ross, we're on a beach."

"Yes, but the soundtrack doesn't have screaming people on it. Anyway, I'm trying to find... ah, there it is.

Amazonian rainforest sounds. Birds and so on."

Harry was aghast. "You're on a beach in England... and you're going to listen to bird noises from Brazil?"

"It's relaxing."

"Fair enough," said Laura. "At least one of us is managing to chill out."

She got up and went to the water's edge. The heat of the sun was on her body, the smell of the salt in her nostrils. Gentle waves ran over her beach sandals and brought her feet to life.

She wondered – was she getting the art of relaxation all wrong?

She set off along the beach, walking along the line where the waves landed. She made a hundred yards east before the shoreline began to curve under the great hill that came to meet it in a rocky hinterland. From above, the whole bay would be visible. Down among the rocks, there was no overview. Only the immediacy of what was coming at her.

Her phone pinged in her shorts.

Do not be Angela.

It was a text from Amy.

'Are you ok?'

She climbed onto a low, flat rock and scoured the beach. There she was – Amy, a little dot, waving by an umbrella. Laura waved back.

She replied to the text.

'Okay, thanks. No need to send a lifeguard.'

A gull landed nearby, but took off again almost immediately. She watched it soar and arc onto a high rocky ledge.

She missed having a loving relationship. She wanted it. She didn't dare trust in finding the fantasy boy though. Not after what had happened with Clive. She stepped down off the rock and enjoyed a wave crashing harmlessly against her legs. She had an ocean of love to give. But no-one to give it to.

9

An Enquiry

#19: Rob Rowlands

Posted 13 years ago

I used to go to Sandy Bay as a kid. My family went with a family from our street in Bristol, maybe because I was an only child (boy) and they had a girl, also an only child, who was a year older than me. Great when we were 4 and 5. Great when we were 10 and 11. Weird when we were 15 and 16. She looked like a woman while I was skinny. I think our parents thought it might become a great love story but I just grew scared of her. Not because she was scary. Quite the opposite. She was gorgeous. All the older boys started to talk to her, especially when she was at the pool. I think the experience gave me an inferiority complex, lol. I'd plucked up courage to do something the following year, but she went to Spain. I haven't been to the Isle of Wight in over 50 years now, but those early memories − I think about them more and more, especially since I lost Mum. The girl is now a retired head teacher and I see her occasionally in town. We always nod. Seriously, I will never ever forget that last holiday when I saw her topless very briefly as I was passing her family's chalet window. Now we're both in our late sixties and have grandchildren. How time flies.

*

Laura was under the big beach umbrella with Amy and baby Evie, who was sitting between Amy's legs on the sand and playing happily with a blue plastic bucket of water and some sea shell shapes. Amy looked less happy – more tired.

Laura picked up a shell shape, filled it with water, and then poured the water back into the bucket. Evie followed her every move.

"I think she's probably had enough play time," said Amy wearily. "Haven't you, Evie?"

"Play time's over, Evie," said Laura. "We'll come here again though, shall we? Shall we?"

"Ross?" said Amy.

"What's up?" said Ross. He was flat on his back listening to something. Laura took a wild guess that it was the sound of the wind on Mars.

"It's hot and Evie should sleep soon. I'd rather that was back at the chalet."

Ross turned and looked over at his fiancée.

"Why?"

"Because I might be able to grab some sleep too."

"Yes, well, I think we've all had enough for today," said Bev. "We have to build up our beach stamina."

Ross sighed and began to help Amy with the baby stuff. But then he stepped away.

"Actually, Plan B," he said.

"Plan B?" said Amy, struggling to hide her annoyance.

"I'll just squeeze in a quick swim," he said.

Before Amy could say anything, he was heading for the water.

"Let me help you with that," said Laura. But she kept one eye on Ross moving into the sea, beyond the numerous paddlers, and then diving forward and powering away from the shore in a decisive front crawl.

He swam a long way.

Having helped Amy, Laura found herself drawn to the water's edge. Was he swimming out too far?

She lost sight of him. Had he gone under? Were there bad tides out there? Riptides? Cross currents? Undercurrents?

Maybe it was a matter for the lifeguard. At what point did you act?

"That was great," a voice called to her.

She looked several yards to her right, where Ross had emerged from among a group of people playing in the waves. She guessed he must have dived under and come up farther over, and then come back on a parallel line – one she hadn't picked up. She was relieved and annoyed in equal measure.

He came over, dripping wet, and made his way past her back to their base.

"Just working off excess energy," were the words he tossed over his shoulder.

Five minutes later, they were leaving the beach, but Laura felt more unrelaxed than ever. She paused on the promenade.

Clive was history, but the boy fantasy was still out there. It had occurred to her while walking back from the flat rock that, as a grown-up, it would be far better for her to nail this stupid fantasy once and for all.

"I'll catch you up in a bit," she called.

It didn't take long to stroll along Fore Street, beyond

the left turn into Bay Street, and onward, along to the far end.

She halted outside the Moorings café. Looking through the window, the eight or so tables inside appeared to be occupied. Fantasy time was over. Reality was about to sweep in like a tidal surge and…

"Hi," said a young woman in an Isle of Wight T-shirt. She was holding a clipboard and pen. "Would you care to sign our petition? It's to get the local council to extend the summer dog beach ban to cover the next bay. We're trying to bring more visitors to the area and it's a great spot for picnics."

"Yes, of course," said Laura. She signed her name and added her chalet number at Hopton's. "There you go."

She barely got inside the café when a forty-something woman restocking the cold drinks cabinet a few feet away muttered something about 'interfering tourists'. Laura couldn't make out the exact words over the gentle hubbub of customers talking.

"Sorry, have I caused a problem?" she asked.

"Not at all. It's just sometimes I wish visitors wouldn't sign petitions that affect the people who live here."

A wasp buzzed Laura's face. She waved it away.

"I'm actually here to speak to Tracy."

"Oh? That's me. What can I do for you?"

Laura took in the furrowed brow of a naturally friendly face.

"I was speaking to Janie," she said. "She thinks you might be able to help me. It's about the family who used to run the Bayside Café back in the late seventies, early eighties. She said you knew the family."

"Oh, come this way." Tracy led Laura behind the counter for privacy. "I did know them but it was a long time ago. I haven't kept in touch."

"I heard the old man passed away recently."

"Yes, I heard that too."

"Did you know his son?"

"Not really. The legal people would have an address though – assuming there was a will."

Good thinking.

"No… no, I can't go that route. It's nothing to do with a will. It's just something I'm doing that might involve the son."

"Have you tried Facebook, Twitter, Instagram?"

No, because I don't know his name.

"Yes… but no luck. It's just that I'm putting a thing together and he should be included. It's quite important."

She wondered if to ask Tracy for his name, but felt it might come across as weird to say it was important she contacted a man she knew nothing about, including his name.

"I didn't have much to do with them," said Tracy, "but I can ask around, if that's a help."

"Yes, that would be great. Thanks."

"Okay, call in tomorrow. I might have some information for you."

"Great."

"Sorry to have confused you with a tourist. What part of the island are you from?"

"Oh…" *Damn.* "East Cowes."

"Righto. I don't get over there too much."

"No… well… I'm staying with friends locally for a bit."

"You're not working then?"

"Not at the moment."

"You poor thing. We can't live on goodwill long, can we."

"No, I suppose not."

"You don't sound like East Cowes."

Crap.

"My accent? No, I lived in London for many years. I've only recently come back."

"Well, the height of summer's almost here. You shouldn't have too much trouble finding a bit of work."

"No, absolutely. Well, thanks again for your help. And sorry about the petition."

"No, you're alright there. Extending the ban is probably good for business. It's just that I have to walk Mum's Scottie and he's a real beach bum. I'll soon be driving for miles to get him to a dog friendly summer beach."

Laura nodded sympathetically.

"Right, well, thanks again. I'll call in tomorrow then."

"Yep, I'll do what I can. After all, we locals have to look out for each other, don't we."

"Yes, absolutely. Thanks."

Laura left the café feeling more fake than a Gucci handbag she once bought for ten pounds in an East London street market.

10

OMG!

#20: debbiedoolanjones

Posted 12 years ago

The old holiday camp is to be refurbished by the Mainstream Group. It's to be called Martin's Sandy Bay.

Going back a few years, I met a boy there when I was 14. His family was in the chalet opposite. We never spoke beyond hello but he seared himself into my soul that fortnight. The things we got up to in my head – marriage, five children, working hard to get them through university... I can't believe we never spoke properly. I'm now 42 and divorced. Did I miss out on the love of my life? Or was he a useless twit who couldn't or wouldn't talk to me.

Freddie Archer replied 12 years ago

Hello everyone. It's Freddie here again. Glad to see this thread is back to life. I haven't checked it for a year or two. Glad to see someone's bringing the old camp back from the dead too. Seaside holidays are so special.

MARK DAYDY

I love your story, debbiedoolanjones. It sounds to me like he was the one who missed out!

Helen Grossman replied 11 years ago

Goodness me, I found this website looking for anything relating to Sandy Bay back in the 70s. I remember you, Freddie. You were lovely. Who did you love? I'm dying to know. My hubby won't go to the Isle of Wight. It's Portugal or Spain every year xx

*

Sunday morning saw the family up early and on the patio, wading through a variety of breakfasts, from Ross's oat cereal to Harry's eggs and bacon. Above them, the sky was blue from end to end, with the rising sun promising a dazzling Sunday. There was less scent in the air now though, as if everything had been baked dry by the ongoing days of sunshine.

"According to my phone, it could get up to thirty today," said Amy. She turned to Harry with a smile. "That's eighty-six in *ye olde* weather."

Laura was munching toast and watching the new arrivals outside Chalet 45 – a Mum, Dad and teen daughter who had turned up on Saturday evening. The mum brushed something off the daughter's T-shirt. A speck of dirt, no doubt. The daughter, who looked around sixteen, didn't respond. Indeed, she seemed separate from her parents in a way that some teens carry off so well – I'm with you, but not *with you*. Laura could

72

imagine conversations beginning with the daughter insisting they stop treating her like a child.

After breakfast, Laura and her family piled into their oversized car for the trip to Osborne House, the summer retreat of Queen Victoria and Prince Albert – a trip Laura had planned in her head on Day One, Hour One. She was looking forward to mooching around in places she'd seen Victoria inhabit in various TV and movie dramas. She was well aware that after Prince Albert's untimely demise, Victoria made Osborne her permanent home. There was something understandable about that. When Jonathan walked out on her, Laura stayed home a lot and might have endured it better had 'home' been a vast estate on an island miles from anywhere.

The drive there wasn't like an English car journey. With no rain for two weeks and the increasing heat turning the greens to yellows and browns, it felt more like a trip through southern Europe.

"England," said Harry, peering out of the window. "The best country in the world for a holiday."

"You're right there," said Bev. "With weather like this, you can't beat it."

"I remember one time we came," said Amy, "it rained all week."

"That's the luck of the draw," said Harry.

"So you're admitting it's better to book Greece?" said Ross.

"No," Harry insisted. "If the weather's bad, then you just put up with it. There are other ways to enjoy a break without being roasted alive."

Osborne House, situated in East Cowes, was well sign-posted, making the sat-nav redundant – and Laura always felt that 'house' never did it justice; the place was clearly a palace.

Having parked the car, they arrived on foot at the portico entrance, with Bev explaining a thing or two to baby Evie, who was wide-eyed in her papoose strapped to Amy.

"My dad loved coming here. That's your great, great grandad, Evie. His name was Stan and he always said we should soak up as much culture as possible because you didn't get so much of it where we lived between the metal works, the coal depot, and the railway."

Laura had prepaid the tickets and tour, so they spent a little time in the shop while they waited for their guide. Bev quickly identified local jam and wine, plus some Victorian themed plates as gifts to take home. Laura couldn't think about gifts, although a regal coffee mug for Angela was tempting. Instead, she went outside for a peek at the wonderful gardens. It was easy to imagine herself as Victoria... mourning Albert... strolling the estate... listening to birdsong... enjoying the solitude...

"Red squirrel!" cried Harry. "Do you know the Isle of Wight and Scotland are the two main locations in the UK where you can see reds?"

"I seem to recall something about the greys coming over from America," said Laura. "I'm not sure how."

"Budget airlines," said Harry. "No, actually the rich brought them over in Victorian times as fashion accessories for their oversized gardens. There are millions of the little pests now. They've practically wiped out the reds through some plague they spread."

Bev called Harry to look at something, leaving Laura free to walk on a little. Way ahead was the Swiss Cottage, built for Victoria and Albert's children. A walk there would reveal the plants Prince Albert had personally chosen to complete the vast landscaping project. Laura knew all this. She had long been fascinated by Victoria and Albert. She'd read that Albert would stand on the roof of the main house, flag in hand, to direct the gardeners as to where trees should be planted.

She wondered. How would Victoria have felt when she first laid eyes on him? Yelling 'Oh My God!' wasn't likely, so playing it cool would have been her approach. That's how you did it.

And how she must have missed him. Not his flag waving, but their conversations over small things, his closeness, his arms around her...

Her phone pinged.

It was an email from Angela, this time expressing concerns about pricing structure. Laura looked up from the screen. Ross was waving. It was time for their tour of the house.

*

Two hours later, Laura was a most satisfied tourist – having enjoyed this latest tour more than any of those on her previous visits down the years. As usual, she never got to see everything, but the sense of Victoria was all-pervading. When Albert died in 1861, at the age of forty-two, Victoria mourned for the whole of her remaining thirty-nine years, always wearing black as a mark of remembrance and respect. It struck Laura as strange that the British Empire should flourish globally under a queen who never seemed to take much active interest in life beyond the tiny Isle of Wight.

"The Victorians really knew about organization and efficiency," said Ross.

"Definitely," said Harry. "When they sent a boy up a sooty chimney to clean it, they always had a spare kid on standby in case the first one fell and broke his neck."

"That's not what I meant," said Ross.

"We mustn't become fans of selective history," said Harry. "For all the wonderful things the Victorians did, they didn't seem too troubled by child poverty or slavery."

"How about visiting the beach?" said Laura.

Without waiting for confirmation, she waved them to follow her down to Victoria and Albert's private beach, situated a ten-minute walk from the main house.

"If I'd known it was a half-marathon, I'd have booked a taxi," said Harry after fifty yards.

At the beach, they admired Victoria's bathing machine – in reality something akin to an American Old West covered wagon that meant Her Majesty could change into her bathing costume without anyone seeing.

"I wonder what the penalty was for catching sight of the Queen's naked butt," said Harry.

"It's a good job you weren't around in those days," said Bev. "You'd have been locked up in the Tower."

"The water looks inviting," said Laura, imagining Victoria taking a dip. It seemed so perfect a place. So calming. So restful.

"Shall we stay here for lunch? Bev asked.

"I'd rather get back to Sandy Bay," said Harry. "If we stay here too long, we'll end up playing poor people in a TV series."

*

That afternoon, back at the camp, it was proving difficult to agree on a joint course of action. Harry and Bev wanted to sleep. Ross wanted to swim. Amy wanted to walk the baby in the pushchair.

Laura was about to volunteer to go with Amy when

Ross shrugged, sighed and agreed to do the fatherly thing. Laura was still happy to go along but they started arguing about responsibilities so Laura held back. She considered following Bev and Harry's lead in taking a nap but, mercifully, she still felt alive and up for action. She guessed at fifty-two that wouldn't always be the case so she wanted to make the most of it.

At a loose end, she walked solo through the camp, passing the busy, noisy pool, and the teenage girl from Chalet 45. The girl, wearing the tiniest possible bikini, was talking and laughing with a boy in shorts who looked around eighteen. The boy looked interested. Too interested. Laura felt like having a word, but held her tongue.

At the back gate, Laura turned right up the hill that jutted out to form the east side of the bay. At the top, she beheld the grand vista of the sea, the beach, the village, the estuary, and the hill that jutted out to form the opposite side of the bay. People were milling around, at play, at rest, having fun. All those lives, all those stories. What dramas, what joys were being experienced by those taking time away from their regular lives? Did any of them look up to the woman on the hill and wonder what was going on *there*? Or was that it – that we see so much and yet so little?

Oh go and have some fun, girl! You're fifty-two, not ninety-two!
She headed down the hill.

A few minutes later, she was taking in the view of the beach from the promenade and promising herself a cold beer if she was still in the village at four.

In the meantime, she got out of the heat by looking in shops for gift ideas, books or anything else that caught her eye. She eventually bought a summer blouse that was much lighter than a couple of the tops she'd packed.

Weather-wise, it was increasingly becoming more like the Isle of Crete than the Isle of Wight.

Then she found herself at the end of Fore Street by the Moorings café. It seemed ridiculous to hide from Tracy, so she popped in with the intent of telling her that the missing boy mystery had been resolved.

"Hi, you're in luck," said Tracy before Laura could utter a word. "I texted my brother and he knew the original owner's son. He'll put you straight. I'll just ping him again."

"I'd hate to put him out," said Laura, but Tracy pulled out her phone and sent a text.

Laura wanted to say how it was all a mistake, but her curiosity had grown. Why walk away? In a few minutes she would know the whereabouts of the boy. Maybe he'd be in Australia and she could enjoy a whole new world of fantasies.

Tracy's phone pinged. She checked it.

"Come on, the laptop's in the back room."

Laura followed her past the end of the counter and the sandwich preparation area.

Through an arch lay a bright, airy kitchen to the right. They turned left, into a drab room that served as both office and storage space. There was a laptop open on a cluttered desk. Tracy fired up the video call link and, within seconds, Laura was sitting in front of a topless man in a bright, white room. She was struck first by his friendly smile and second by the fact he looked around her own age.

If we were the last two people on Earth, then possibly…

"Hi, you must be Laura. I'm Matt."

Forget the last two people clause…

"Hi."

"Tracy says you're trying to track down Dave

Williams. Last I heard he was living in Southampton with a wife and two teenage kids. I expect they're grown up by now. Did you know Dave well?"

"Not as such. I just know he used to help his parents in the Bayside Café."

And I've had a lifelong fantasy thing going on which we won't discuss...

"Yeah, just one thing wrong with that, Laura. Dave never helped out in the café on account of him being the laziest little so-and-so on the island. It was me who used to help out – for pocket money, obviously."

Laura was astonished.

"You? Oh my God!"

11

Now What?

#21: Foreman Christopher

Posted 11 years ago

I'm studying sociology for a degree and I'm researching life away from the workplace and the home. This site has given me a plethora of information. I can see how working class people would have felt 'at home' in these large holiday camps, whereas Community Spirit isn't necessarily something the middle class would seek out when taking a break. It's given me some great ideas for work on social cohesion.

Captain Pugwash replied 11 years ago

Get a life.

*

Laura fidgeted in the chair.

It's him. The boy! And he's topless!

She studied his fanciable face and neat, darkish hair. She thought of doing something with her own locks but

80

didn't, leaving her hand in mid-air.

"Um, so… Matt…" *Think of something to say!* "Thanks for clarifying that point about Dave. I'm guessing you're working in a different part of the island, are you?"

Where are my car keys?

"No, I'm in Spain."

"Spain?"

Okay, so he's in a different country.

"Yeah, look, I might be able to get an address for Dave if it's important. Is it important?"

"Yes, it's important."

"No problem. We islanders have to stick together. Tracy says you're from East Cowes."

"Yes, that's right."

Okay, so he's in Spain and I'm a fake islander. How's this going to work?

"Okay," said Matt, "I'll text a couple of people who might know his current details. Call in to Tracy tomorrow. I'm off now. See you, Laura."

Matt slipped his sunglasses on and exited the call.

He's married. Definitely married. Thirty years married. Ten kids.

Laura turned to Tracy. "Does he work in Spain?"

Tracy laughed. "No, he's on holiday with his mates."

"Oh right."

I am a spy and I need information.

"So his… wife doesn't mind?"

"No, he's one hundred percent single."

"Right, well…" *Single. Very good.* "I'll um…"

"Pop in tomorrow?"

"Yes. Great. Thanks again."

Laura exited the café. She needed to walk somewhere, anywhere, and put some distance between herself and Matt. Although – wasn't he already a thousand miles away? Would an extra few yards make any difference? The situation was certainly an odd one.

Yes, she fancied him.

Yes, he was at a different holiday location.

Yes, it was stupid.

Yes, she was acting like a teenager.

She paused.

Surely this was doomed from the start. A nice idea, but really, really stupid. She was a grown woman. She was a granny, for God's sake. And she had sent Matt off to find some guy called Dave, whoever the hell he was.

And there was the other problem. He was on holiday with his mates. That would mean loads of strong booze and easy sex, no doubt.

Unless he was there to look at historical monuments.

Did Matt like historical monuments?

No! This wasn't going to happen. She simply had an updated version of the boy-man in her Isle of Wight fantasy.

End of.

Laura reached the jetty where she realized she'd been humming the old song, 'Walking Back To Happiness'. She ordered herself to stop acting like a love-struck idiot. Meeting Matt was a million-to-one shot that merely signified that the boy she rarely thought about was now a man in Spain having a good time with several loose women.

Would he give up that lifestyle for a woman who pretended to be from East Cowes?

On the still water, a boat coming in caused all the other boats to bob up and down in its wake. She recalled being fifteen and standing on this very spot, taking in this very scene, and wishing she could get something going with the boy.

She walked back through the village, stopping to buy a mint-choc ice cream cone to give herself something to do while she put Matt out of her mind. Having fun wasn't as easy as some people made out. There were traps. At the end of the day, Sandy Bay was just another business location and she was a fifty-two-year-old grandmother. There was no magic at work here.

She reached the promenade behind the beach.

Clive.

He was on one of the benches with his phone to his ear. Beside him was an upturned straw hat.

Fun?

It was too tempting.

As she passed behind the bench, she leaned over and knocked the scoop of ice-cream off her cone into the hat. A small girl was watching in amazement. Then the man who had been tying the small girl's shoe laces – her father, probably – retrieved his hat and put it on. Only he stopped and froze. In some ways, literally.

Laura hurried away eating the remainder of the evidence. She would avoid Tracy and get back to what she had come to Sandy Bay for – a relaxing break.

12

Hello Again

#22: Freddie Archer

Posted 10 years ago

Hello everyone. It's Freddie here again. I must apologize to Helen Grossman who replied a year ago to my comment of two years ago. It's the first time I've looked here in a long while (despite contributing a number of times in the past). Thanks for your kind comment, Helen. I remember you too! You worked very hard behind the scenes, doing reception and smoothing over customer issues. As for who I loved? Life moves on. I had my chance but failed to act. I wouldn't dream of naming names now and causing possible embarrassment. Those were very happy days though. By the way, it's completely understandable that you should choose Spain and Portugal for the fantastic weather. If only we could guarantee that much sunshine in Britain!

*

The following morning, around eleven, Laura and her family were enjoying coffee in the holiday park's pavilion.

It was busy and a little noisy, but Laura was happy spending time with her loved ones, even if she was still tired from a restless night in a stuffy bedroom that wasn't aided by eating far too much at the Bayview Pizzeria. The pavilion thankfully was bright and airy, its faux leather chairs were comfy, people were chatting or staring at their phones, and the vibe was cheerful.

Not for the first time, she thought of Matt.

And of Matt in Spain.

And of a bunch of men in their early fifties drinking too much beer and getting up to no good.

Then she thought of her real mission – to simply recharge her batteries before returning to London.

"This is the way to spend a Monday," said Ross.

"Fed up at work then?" Harry asked.

"When did I say I was fed up at work?"

"It creeps up on you," Harry insisted. "One day you're in the tax office thinking something's not quite right, the next you're storming out yelling 'I will not bully small taxpayers!' You should be careful. How are you going to pay the mortgage if you quit your job?"

"I'm perfectly happy at work, thanks, Harry."

"It's going to be another lovely day," said Amy. "According to my phone, we'll hit thirty again. That's eighty-six, Harry."

"I don't know how these people do it," said Bev. She was indicating a couple of orange coats who were juggling tennis balls for a small group of fascinated young children.

"I don't think I could spend all day trying to make people happy," said Harry.

"Have you thought of just starting with a minute or two?" Ross suggested.

"They do a wonderful job," said Bev.

"According to the website, there are twenty-five of them," said Amy.

"That's quite a few," said Bev.

"Not really," said Ross. "You've got three thousand people staying at the camp."

"Park," said Bev. "Somebody told me they don't like you calling it a camp. It's a holiday park."

"It says here they earn around fifteen thousand a year," said Amy, checking her phone. "Twenty for the more senior ones."

"That's not much," said Ross.

"No, but they get free accommodation and subsidized food."

"I imagine they make lots of good friends," said Bev. "Working and living together does that."

"I wonder who makes the orange jackets," said Harry. "That would be a good little business. Especially if they make the blue coats for Pontin's and red ones for Butlin's…"

Laura spotted a lost child. She couldn't prove it, but she saw the little boy looking up at faces in an ever more desperate search for familiarity. She was about to move into action when a female orange coat came swiftly to the rescue. Comforting words and simple questions stopped the child's lower lip from wobbling. Then they went to the disco DJ's microphone where a request for the boy's mum, Molly, was issued to come and claim the lovely little Robin. Molly was soon hurrying across the dance floor to scoop up her son. Laura approved. Hopton's had this sort of thing covered. If only one of their orange coats would realize she was looking for someone too.

She shook herself out of it. She was there for fun and relaxation.

"Okay, hands up," said Harry. "Who's ever had a

holiday romance?"

His question was met with disbelief.

"I don't need all the sordid details," he said. "I'm just asking who's ever fallen in love with someone while on a summer holiday?"

"Is this a confession waiting to happen, Harry?" Ross asked.

"You go first."

"There's nothing to tell."

"Of course there is. You're a man, right? Even if it was someone who never realized you existed."

"Okay, well…" Ross seemed to be weighing up whether or not this was a particularly good idea. "I once went to Malta with my family and developed a liking for a girl staying at our hotel. I used to wait for her to go out with her family then I'd accidentally be going the same way."

"Isn't that stalking?" Harry wondered aloud. "Unless the girl was under age, then it's a more serious crime."

"She was sixteen like me," Ross insisted. "Anyway, we did manage to find a little time together but it was all quite innocent."

"And that's it?" said Harry, sounding disappointed.

"That's it," Ross confirmed.

"Mine was with an underage boy," said Laura. "He was around eleven and so was I."

She was about to tell them how this great love had nearly come roaring back into her life. But she couldn't.

*

The family decided to put off a trip to the model village for a couple of hours. Instead, Laura was outvoted as they plumped for a stroll into the village to look at the boats and grab some lunch.

As they passed Hopton's hectic pool, a young female orange coat came over to make a fuss of Evie, pulling silly faces and doing a little dance. The baby laughed and gurgled.

"You guys do such a brilliant job," said Laura. "It must be hard work."

"As long as I start with coffee and a banana, I'm fine. I love meeting guests and making sure you all have an enjoyable stay."

"Well, thank you for what you do, Fliss," said Laura, having checked her name badge.

"Yes," said Bev. "Your parents must be very proud of you."

Fliss went off to engage with another family and Laura thought that making people happy wouldn't be the worst thing anyone could do for a living.

Her phone pinged.

She checked the screen.

Speaking of bringing joy...

It was an email from Angela relating to client feedback as a driver of continuous improvement and sustainable change. Laura replied positively but briefly, along the lines of all Angela's suggestions being sensible. She only wished the same word could apply to the stuff churning around in her head.

She was a sensible person at heart, of course – no doubt about it. She had worked in education long before taking a role with Angela. She'd also raised a daughter and handled a demanding husband for twenty years. So why had she been handed a stupid fate? She hadn't closed her heart down, but why did such a viable candidate for her love have to be a fantasy figure from the past who was only available over the internet?

She wondered. What would be the sensible thing to do?

*

Their stroll eventually brought them to the far end of Fore Street, where Laura stopped outside the Moorings café. Tracy was inside, restocking the drinks cooler. Bev and Harry had stopped to look in a window a little way back. Amy, Ross and Evie were over by a beachwear place checking out the sandals and flip-flops. Laura was torn. Despite her insightful self-analysis and deconstruction of the situation, she found that something almost magnetic was drawing her in.

"Hi," said Tracy, suddenly at the doorway. "Still unemployed?"

"Oh… er, yes," said Laura. "It's fine though. No problem at all."

"You couldn't help me out, could you?" Tracy asked. "I'm up to my neck in staff shortages."

Laura stared back at her as if she were speaking Ancient Greek, but Tracy had to get back behind the counter to serve a fresh customer.

"Just for two days?" she implored. "It's good pay, Laura. We locals have to look out for each other, don't we?"

A silver-haired elderly woman hobbled in from the back of the café followed by an old Scottie dog.

"I'll take that break now, Tracy."

"This is Laura, Mum. The woman I told you about."

"Oh hello, Laura," said Tracy's mum. That was the cue for the Scottie to bustle over for a bit of fuss.

"Hello doggy," said Laura bending down in the doorway to scratch an ear.

"That's Bonzo," said Tracy. "He's an attention seeker. My mum's Liz. Also an attention seeker."

Laura smiled at Liz and enjoyed the smell of the dog and its soft tongue trying to lick her hand.

"Right, I'll be going up," said Liz. "Nice to meet you, Laura."

"You too," said Laura, getting to her feet.

Slowly, the old lady made her way out to the back followed by the dog.

"My mum," said Tracy. "She'll be fighting fit in a couple of days. She jarred her back. Could I please persuade you to help out? Just a couple of days until Mum's back eases up. We've got to look after our mums, haven't we?"

"Yes," said Laura, agreeing about looking after mums.

"Oh, I can't tell you how much I appreciate it, Laura. I really can't."

Er...?

"I've got a family thing," she said. "This afternoon."

"Brilliant. Be here tomorrow at half-twelve. It's lunches and cream teas, so I only need you till half-four. Three days at the absolute most. Oh, listen to me rambling on – you're wondering how my brother got on. Let's try him, shall we?"

Matt?

Laura didn't want to work in a café. She did want to see Matt though.

Three minutes later, she was staring at him on Tracy's laptop. Thankfully, he was wearing a T-shirt.

"Hi Laura."

"Hi..."

Laura's brain was racing but getting nowhere. Wasn't it time to explain that the whole thing was an error? Or did having fun mean she should carry on regardless?

Tracy leaned in. "Laura's helping me out in the café for a few days. Until Mum's fit again."

"That's great, Laura," said Matt. "You're an absolute star."

"No, it's just… for a very brief time. No time at all, really."

"I'll leave you to it," said Tracy as she made her way out to the counter.

"So, Laura, you're in Sandy Bay to… what exactly?"

"I was just trying to find out a few things."

"Any reason?"

"It relates to…" *What does it relate to?* "…a family history I'm writing."

"Oh? Who'd want to read Dave's family history?"

"A distant relative."

So distant he's invisible.

"So you're a writer," said Matt. "That must be interesting."

Laura swallowed drily. She hated lying. She was also feeling hot, although that was probably the weather.

"It's mainly…" *Mainly what?* "…family history, ghost writing articles, novels. None of it under my name, so you won't find anything on Google. And I have to sign confidentiality contracts, so I can't tell you anything."

"And I can't tell you anything either. I'm still waiting for people to get back to me about Dave's whereabouts. You can tell me about you though. I assume that's not subject to contract?"

"No…"

"I'm guessing writing doesn't pay well?"

"Why would you say that?"

"You're working in my family's café at ten percent over minimum wage."

"Ah well, yes… about that…" *Tell him he was the boy,*

91

then flee.

"It's important that islanders stick together. Have we seen you in Sandy Bay before this writing job?"

"Oh… when I was young. With my dad. When he was on business. I'm talking about the late seventies, early eighties."

"Great days."

"I used to go to the Bayside café during the summer. You were the boy."

"The boy?"

"The boy who served me when I was eleven, thirteen, fourteen, fifteen… I don't suppose you remember?"

She knew it wasn't likely.

"As you know, the island gets thousands of people coming through every café every week during the summer."

"Of course."

Matt broke into a big smile. "I'm surprised you remember me from all that time ago. Did you fancy me?"

"What?"

"Or maybe I spilled tea on you?"

"No, never. The tea or…"

"Only it usually takes something out of the ordinary to stick in our minds at that age."

"Yes."

"So, what stuck in your mind?"

"What stuck in my mind?"

"Yes, what stuck in your mind?"

"Oh, it's probably just the golden glow of youth, I expect. Silly really."

"Well, you seem a really lovely person, Laura. I must have been a right twit not to get to know you back then."

"Ah well, that's life."

"Okay, well, I'd better get going. I'm due on the golf

course in an hour."

"Okay, it was nice talking to you, Matt."

"Same here."

After the call, Laura had a ton of questions for Tracy. She just wasn't sure if to ask any of them, bearing in mind that she wouldn't be coming back to work in the café. After all, she was on holiday.

Then again, if she wanted to get to know the boy who had become the man, would a day or two helping Tracy be so onerous?

"Will he help out here when he gets back from Spain?" she asked.

Yes, clever Laura – nice and neutral.

"No," said Tracy. "He'll go straight back to Warwick."

"Warwick?"

The wrong side of England! Still…

"He's a psychiatrist in a practice there."

"Really?" Laura grasped for positives.

A second chance to live out my fantasy, and this time it's with a psychiatrist!

"Yes, he's a bright boy," said Tracy.

Laura felt weird. Was there an established pattern of serious-minded psychiatry professionals falling for middle-aged fake authors who pretended to be from the Isle of Wight? Or were such encounters limited to therapy sessions on the clinic couch?

"Does he often go off like that with his friends?" she asked.

"This one's to celebrate a mate's fiftieth birthday. They grew up together, so he's now trapped on Planet Robbie. That's the guy who's fifty – only his planet's not somewhere you'd want to be trapped."

Laura tried to block a vivid picture forming in her mind.

"Poor Matt. It sounds bad."

"Yeah, as long as he doesn't get drunk. Then things can seem less hellish."

Laura mentally stepped away. Decades had passed since she last played the role of party animal. Ibiza 1986 came to mind, but not in a good way.

"So," said Tracy, "did I hear you're writing a family history?"

"Ah yes – although I can't talk about it on account of the contract I signed."

And the fact it's all a big fat lie.

13

Life in Miniature

#23. Toby T.

Posted 10 years ago

I went to Hopton's Sandy Bay four times as a kid and loved it. I always wished I could live there. I have some lovely photos too. Back then, they had an official photographer wandering around, especially in the evening. Next day, you would go to the big boards in reception and try to see if you were in any of the hundreds of photos. You could buy the normal paper photo or, better still, you could buy one as a tiny slide and they'd put it inside a little plastic keyring tube so you could see yourself by holding it up to the light. I've still got one of me aged 7. I look so happy. We were so so so lucky that out parents worked hard to give us those holidays. Thanks mum and dad xx.

*

The Monday afternoon journey to Godshill Model Village was going well. They were halfway through the ten-mile car journey and all were in good spirits.

"Wonderful countryside," said Harry as they drove by a couple of workers in a field.

"You're not wrong," said Bev, "although it looks a bit parched."

"People don't value outdoor work enough, these days," said Harry. "Outdoor people are lucky. They get to experience the seasons."

"Try telling them that in February," said Ross.

"The thing is," Harry continued, "up until a few generations ago, most people worked in agriculture. That meant they spent all day outside. There was an article in the paper recently that said exposing ourselves to brighter outdoor light makes us happier."

They were passing two young people kissing at a rural bus stop.

"You're right," said Ross.

At Godshill's model village, they parked the car, made sure Evie was well watered, and went inside.

"Isn't it lovely," said Bev, taking in the miniature recreations of local villages as they were in the 1920s and 30s.

Laura concurred and anticipated a trip down memory lane might be imminent.

"Villages had more character back then," said Harry. "You didn't need to be on Facebook to know what was going on. They had the grapevine."

"Shame they haven't got a model-sized holiday camp," said Bev.

"Did you know the first Butlin's red coat was a man called Norman Bradford?" said Harry.

"Yes," said Ross.

That surprised Laura – and Harry too.

"When Billy Butlin opened his first camp in Skegness," Ross continued, "he found his guests didn't get involved in the activities. So he asked his engineer, an outgoing guy called Norman Bradford, to engage them with *ice-breakers*. Everyone had a great time, giving Billy Butlin the idea that if he had a hundred Norman Bradfords…"

Harry stared at Ross.

"How do you know all that?"

"Wikipedia. I anticipated it would come in handy."

While Harry went on to extol the virtues of the old days and old ways, Laura's mind entered the miniature world of Godshill where miniature police were attempting to arrest a miniature woman for pretending to be from East Cowes and telling lies to a psychiatrist because he once served her a cream tea.

"This wouldn't be my first choice of holiday activity," said Ross.

"What's wrong with it?" said Harry.

"Nothing – it's just… well, there are other holiday activities that younger people find interesting."

"Such as?"

"Kiteboarding, tubing, zorbing, blokarting, skijoring…"

"I didn't know you spoke Norwegian."

"I'm talking about adventure, adrenaline…"

Laura was now in a mini court facing a mini judge. He sentenced her to three hundred cream teas with Clive.

*

Back at Hopton's at five, a little tired from their exertions, and with baby Evie sound asleep, they were enjoying a cuppa with a slice of chocolate cake. Although the chit-chat was on the likely places they might visit over the coming days, Laura had no trouble understanding the look Ross was secretly giving Amy. Amy's statement a moment later came as no surprise.

"I think me and Ross might grab an hour's sleep while Evie's quiet."

She picked up the carry seat and followed Ross into their room.

Laura turned off the part of her brain that knew what was coming next.

"Why can't they fall asleep on the sofa like normal people?" said Harry.

"That might prove embarrassing," said Bev. "Anyway, we could do with a little relaxation too. Come on."

"I'm not tired," said Harry.

"Yes, you are," said Bev. "Come on."

Harry shrugged and followed.

A moment later the main room was silent. Even so, Laura went out onto the patio as she feared hearing anyone sleeping.

Above her, the sun was beginning to think about getting lower in the sky, but it was still incredibly warm.

Her phone pinged.

Hi Laura

How about this for the website?

DEAR SCHOOL LEADER. BEFORE YOU TALK TO US:

1. Do you know what you want the training to achieve? Think about the outcome you want. Can you set specific objectives? Will staff have a robust understanding of what they will achieve?

2. Do you already have the right person on your staff to deliver the course? If so, will they have

time to prepare? If not, talk to us and we'll find the right person for you. The main thing is that those attending the training respect the person delivering it.

3. Do you have a good learning space that isn't hot or cold, stuffy or badly lit? We all do better in light and airy conditions.

Any thoughts? I'd like to put it up this week.

Laura looked up from her screen and tried to analyze the situation like an adult or, perhaps, a psychiatrist. She saw Matt as the kind of man she might forge the beginnings of a relationship with – if only he wasn't on Planet Robbie in Spain. On the other hand, she knew all this holiday romance nonsense wasn't really worth the bother. There was no depth to a holiday entanglement. It was all heart flutters and heat. Lots of heat.

Yes, but…

The idea that she might see Matt when he returned to England had to be worth thinking about. She understood how she was currently falling for an online version of him – so God knows what he'd be like in real life – but it had to be worth a try, didn't it?

Or would it be best to forget video calls and remain in the bosom of her family? Well, sitting outside while the rest of her family were in each other's bosoms.

She could see ahead to midnight – she'd be in bed alone in a stuffy room with no air conditioning. She'd have plenty of time to consider all aspects of her best way forward, including all aspects of Matt – both real and fantasy.

She studied her screen again. Maybe Angela was on to something.

Think about the outcome you want.

She thought of Sandy Bay as a miniature village and she placed Matt in a mini plane and flew him in to the mini airport she had just created. Then they were together and...

And what?

Ross emerged.

He looked frustrated.

"I'm going for a walk," he huffed.

Watching him go, Laura accepted it was none of her business. All the same, she would use the remainder of the holiday to get to the bottom of it, because, for some reason, it all looked horribly familiar.

14

Part of the Team

#24: thackers

Posted 10 years ago

Hi everyone. I worked at Sandy Bay in 1977 as a 22-year-old barmaid and became friends with many lovely people there. I know of three who have since passed away and I'm sorry to see the camp has had some ups and downs. I'm a nurse nowadays, although I'll be retiring soon. I often think of those sunny far off days. Must be a dreamer xx

> Freddie Archer replied 10 years ago
>
> Hello everyone. It's Freddie here again. Thackers, welcome to the Dreamers Club. Glad to hear you made lots of friends back in those far off days. It really was a special place to meet lovely people.

*

The following day at lunchtime, Laura felt absolutely ridiculous turning up at the café. Tracy was busy with a customer but gave her a beaming smile of friendship, and no doubt relief.

"Hot enough for you?" her new boss asked.

Laura puffed out her cheeks. The air was thick with the aromas of fried bacon, fresh coffee, and sunscreen melting into sweaty bodies. With the temperature set to soar into the thirties – or nineties as Harry's would have it – she expected working conditions to be a challenge if it got really busy. Would fainting put customers off their apple turnovers?

On top of all that, Laura had endured a sleepless night thanks to the heat and a late Thai restaurant meal that brought on indigestion.

She fought off a yawn.

"Didn't sleep too well," she said as soon as Tracy had finished with the customer. "Late restaurant meal with my family."

"Celebration was it?"

"Pardon?"

"The family going out on a Monday night?"

Probably best not to say we're holidaymakers.

"Yes… a birthday."

"Oh, Tess is with us," said Tracy, changing the subject. "She's serving out the back. And I promise that Mum will be back at work within two days, even if I have to plug her into the nearest socket."

Laura smiled. Tracy seemed a really solid, dependable type weighed down by a bit of back luck.

"Perhaps you should show me the ropes," she suggested.

"Right, brilliant, and thank you again. All the prices are up on the board, but also by the till and card reader. Takeaways are self-explanatory, but customers eating in order and pay at the counter and then go grab a table.

They get a receipt with a number which is copied for the preparation area, so if you're not sure which table they're at, just call out the number. Most importantly, the staff bathroom is up those stairs by the back door. Um... that's it."

"No problem."

Tracy handed her a lightweight tabard, catering hat, and makeshift name badge. Unexpectedly, Laura felt part of the team.

"Oh, I must remember to refill the water bowl," said Tracy. "We have one out the back for dogs."

"That's nice," said Laura.

"We love dogs here."

"Yes, I've met Bonzo."

"Yeah, a nice little fella. Loyal, but smells a bit."

"I had a boyfriend like that," a middle-aged woman declared. She had come in from the outdoor area at the back carrying a haphazard stack of used crockery, although Laura's gaze was on her bright green hair, black eye liner and pale pink lip gloss.

"Laura, meet Tess. Tess... Laura."

"Hello," said Laura.

"Hiya," said Tess. "Don't fall into Tracy's trap. I said I'd do two days – I've been here two years. Drug dealers get shorter sentences."

Laura wasn't sure what to say, but Tess disappeared into the kitchen.

"Laura," said Tracy, handing her a slip with the number 242 on it. "Could you make up this order and take it outside."

While Tracy dealt with fresh customers, Laura went to the preparation area behind the counter, donned her uniform, and made up the order: 1 x cheddar cheese & mustard pickle sandwich; 1 x iced orange juice. It did occur to her that Tracy and Tess ought to be able to manage the situation between them but then Tracy disappeared through an internal doorway opposite the counter. Armed with order 242, Laura glanced through the doorway on her way to the outdoor area. It was the souvenir shop next door. Tracy was in there, behind the counter, serving a customer!

What?

"All go, ennit?" said Tess, bustling back the other way with more dirty plates and cups.

Laura realized she hadn't worked alongside anyone as brash as Tess since her volunteer days at a pre-school playgroup twenty-five years ago. That had been Loudmouth Lindy, who used to tell Laura all her business whether she wanted to hear it or not. Prior to that, it would have been a few of the girls she preferred to avoid during her schooldays. It seemed a harsh assertion though. Tess was probably the salt of the earth.

Laura stepped outside.

The half full *al fresco* dining area was a fair size, not only extending a good sixty feet from the building, but also running across the back of both the café and the souvenir shop. There were a dozen or so round tables under yellow umbrellas that could seat four – or five at a pinch – for breakfast, lunch, or a cream tea. There were also a few smaller tables, ideal for couples, dotted around the edges and in the outer corners. Every so often were pots blooming with geraniums, lobelias and other bright flowers.

Still feeling odd at being on the other side of the worker-tourist equation, Laura announced herself.

"Order two-four-two, please?"

A woman, possibly in her mid-seventies, waved from a nearby table.

"Um… one cheese and pickle sandwich and one iced orange juice," Laura announced meekly upon arrival. She wondered if she should put more oomph into it, but supposed she wasn't on stage at the Old Vic, so it was probably fine.

"Thank you," said the cheese and pickle lady, looking a little hot and bothered. Perhaps she didn't need to wear a cardigan in this heat.

Faced with her first ever customer, Laura decided to be the ultimate professional.

"Are you having a good stay?" she asked.

"Yes, thank you."

"The weather's hot, isn't it."

"Yes, very hot."

"Right, well…"

"I'm sorry," said the woman, "you wouldn't believe I used to be good at talking to people."

"Oh, no problem. Have you visited many places? Tourist attractions, I mean."

"No, I only arrived at the weekend… Laura."

Laura's alarm rose up… and then receded.

The name badge.

"I've booked the hotel for two weeks, though," the woman said, "so I should be able to fit in a fair few visits – starting tomorrow at Osborne House."

"Oh brilliant. We were there on Sunday. It's so lovely."

"It's good to know local people visit the attractions, not just us tourists."

"Oh er… yes, absolutely. Um, let me know if you need anything else."

Laura picked up some dirty cups and plates from another table and headed back inside.

Tracy's mum, Liz, was at the foot of the stairs.

"I just wanted to come down and say thank you, Laura. You're a real Godsend."

"It's just a bit of help, that's all."

"Well, we're very grateful. I hope we can help you at some point."

Despite Liz's years, Laura found herself looking into a radiant, still beautiful face.

"It's no problem at all, Liz. But um... the souvenir shop?"

Laura indicated the door just a few feet away into the adjoining premises.

"Yes, that's ours too. Janet runs it for us, but she has to have breaks. Pop your head in... Janet, this is Laura..."

Laura exchanged hellos with a woman in her sixties.

"So, this is out little empire," Liz continued. "I'm sure you can see how our lunches and afternoon cream teas make it impossible for Tracy and Tess to cover everything. I'll be alright soon enough though."

Liz went back upstairs while Laura dropped the used crockery by the kitchen sink and attended to a customer at the counter. It felt strange being at work while on holiday – but then she supposed Angela wouldn't see it like that.

15

What's Love Got To Do With It?

#25: Lewis Phillips

Posted 9 years ago

I remember staying at Hopton's holiday camp in Sandy Bay a few times when I was young, around 1978-86. We stayed in other holiday camps too (in Devon, mainly). The one thing I recall more than anything is how much time me and my two brothers spent outdoors. We literally went out in the morning, teamed up with a few other lads, and stayed out all day long. I work in an office now and I'm sure being stuck inside affects me negatively. Could someone please bring back the good old days.

Freddie Archer replied 9 years ago

Hello everyone. Freddie here again. Lewis, I sympathize with you about office work. Great memories of being out all day. That was quite normal back then, wasn't it. Happy days.

*

Around half-two, when the lunchtime trade had finally died down, Tess took Laura to the large fridge in the preparation area.

"Right, from around three, it'll be cream teas all the way," she said.

She took a large tub of cream as thick as butter from the fridge to a worktop beside it and showed Laura how to fill up the individual portion ceramic pots.

"Fill me with your cream, baby," she sang softly.

Laura's eyes widened in mild horror. Thankfully, the few customers they had were all outside.

Is she for real?

Next, Tess grabbed a large jam jar and a spoon to make up small jam pots.

"You ever had this stuff licked off you?" she asked.

Laura's expression must have answered for her.

"Very wise," said Tess. "It takes forever."

"I don't doubt it."

"Yeah, and God help you if a wasp flies in through the window."

Laura tried not to imagine it, but failed.

"I broke four ornaments and two ribs," said Tess. She then indicated the small, filled pots. "So, it's one of each plus two small scones, two fresh strawberries and a few blueberries. Plus their hot drink – that's one serving."

"Right, got it."

"Make up a good few pots in advance while it's quiet – that's my advice. When it gets busy later, just pull them from the fridge. If you try to do it all on the hoof, you'll find yourself making a right mess."

A while later, having made up a few dozen pots, Laura set to cleaning the vacant indoor tables. She wanted to make sure everything was sparkling for the cream tea rush. Only her heart was suddenly in her mouth. Just outside, Amy was fussing over Evie. What was she doing here? This was a tiny part of the Isle of Wight. How could her daughter be standing the other side of the window?

Laura calmed herself.

Obviously, Amy was waiting for Ross.

Ross... where was that boy and why couldn't he take Amy to watch him snofarting or whatever the hell it was he liked doing? Actually, why couldn't he snuggle up with her at the chalet? Fear rose up in her bosom again. What if they came in? How was that going to work? Would she just play it cool? Kind of – *Oh hi Amy, hi Ross. Cream tea for two, is it?*

Plainly, that wouldn't work at all.

Hide!

She did so – in the souvenir shop next door.

"Um... hi, Janet."

"Oh hello, Laura. You couldn't cover for me, could you? I'm dying to pop upstairs."

"Oh... right. Yes."

"You don't need to do anything. Just make sure no-one runs off with all the stock or money."

"Yes... of course."

"I'll only be a minute."

As Janet disappeared through an interior door at the back, the front door swung open and Amy and Evie came in.

Laura ducked below the counter.

Hurry up, Janet!

An ice age passed and then the front door opened again.

"You're not buying any of this, are you?" said Ross.

"I'm just having a look," said Amy. "Stop nitpicking all the time."

Laura was adamant. There was no way this could work. She was on the Isle of Wight for ten days of relaxation, even if on her fifth day she still didn't feel very relaxed and had now taken a job.

Janet returned.

"Thanks," she said.

Laura nodded and sought the connecting doorway... only Ross stupidly came round that side of the shop.

"Laura?"

"Ross, hi. I just thought... I'd make an early start on the souvenir shopping." She grabbed the nearest object. "Do you think your parents would like a ceramic crab cello player?"

"Mum?" Now Amy was getting involved. "Why are you wearing a name badge... and a catering tabard and hat?"

"I'm just helping someone," said Laura, whizzing away and out through the front door into the street.

Outside, she scuttled a little way along Fore Street and hid in an alley. She stayed there, spying round the corner until she was happy that Amy, Ross and Evie had departed.

Returning to the café, Laura prepared to come clean.

"Ah Tracy..."

"Matt just texted about some family business and asked if you wanted to catch up with him?"

Hot Matt?

"Er... yes. Yes, that would be great."

Laura followed her into the back room, where Tracy's laptop was open. She was soon staring at Matt, who looked cool in a buttery T-shirt. He also carried off the sunglasses on the head thing quite well.

Laura whipped off her catering hat.

"So how's the break going?" she asked.

"Great. We'll be out on the golf course again soon."

"Is that with your friend, Robbie?"

Of Planet Robbie fame.

"Yes, and four others."

"Did he *plan it* like that, did he? Did Robbie *plan it*?"

"Plan what?"

"Lots and lots of… you know… golf."

Of course, it had just dawned on her that golf was a euphemism. Balls, holes… going up the fairway. What a disgusting bunch.

"Yes, it's a golf resort just outside Alicante," said Matt. "We're all golf regulars. Um… on other matters, before I go, nobody knows where Dave went. He doesn't seem to be on social media either."

Laura was torn. Matt didn't come across like an inhabitant of Planet Robbie.

"Let's forget Dave," she said. "He was a red herring."

"Okay, then I suppose we're done."

"Yes, although… a psychiatrist on a jolly boys holiday to Alicante?"

"One of the benefits of the single life at fifty-two. I wasn't quite so happy at forty-two, but I'm in the groove now. How about you? Are you in a relationship?"

"Me? No. As you say, it's good to be free from relationship commitments at our age."

Why did I say that? Help.

"I'm not so sure," said Matt, "but I respect your choice."

What? No.

"Yes…"

Yes?

"You might approve of a paper I once read," said Matt. "It proposes that love doesn't exist, that it's simply the human species protecting itself from extinction via a subconscious process."

"I can't see anyone putting that on a Valentine's Day card."

"They should. A fair percentage of the population is made up of cynics."

"You don't believe it, do you…? That love doesn't exist?"

"It's from a science paper. It's not about belief."

"Ah."

"According to this paper, it's all about lust, attraction, and attachment."

"Lust…"

Calm down, Laura.

"It proposes that a biological imperative has so invaded our thought processes that we believe love is real, when in fact this imperative has employed hormones and chemicals to trick us."

"Right, so that's the end of the candlelit dinner then."

"No, I'd fight them on that one. They might come at me armed with papers pointing to the power of dopamine, adrenaline, and norepinephrine, but I'd fire a champagne cork to hold them off."

"That's a very romantic image," said Laura, imagining it.

"Personally, I think love can stand up for itself," said Matt, "whether we're deluding ourselves or not."

"That's nice to hear."

"It's just that you and I have opted out."

Have we?

"Yes, we have, Matt. We've outwitted that imperative. Well done us."

Laura felt something. Matt was in the wrong country and yet she wanted to get to know him more. On the plus side, if more video calls merely revealed another creep, she could ditch him with one click.

"Well, I should be going," said Matt.

He's going. Possibly forever. Think of something, you idiot.

"I'm writing a novel."

"Are you?"

Am I?

"Yes." Laura's throat constricted. "It's about a main character."

"They often are."

"Well, two main characters. I'm still working on them."

"I hope it goes well."

"You must have some experience of people."

"Yes, I've met some."

"I mean a deeper understanding. That's what I'm trying to do – show off the deeper side of the human experience."

"I'm no expert when it comes to writing fiction. They say you should write what you know, although I'm not so sure that's particularly helpful. Let me think... okay, so you write about what happens to fictional people. Do you write about your own experiences through your characters?"

"No, the main female character..." *Who is she? What does she do?* "...she's into diving. I've never tried that."

"You've never dived?" Matt seemed surprised. "Even though you're from East Cowes?"

"Um...?"

"It's full of boats by the sea?"

"Oh right. No, I've never dived."

"So, is writing about it expressing a bottled-up urge, perhaps?"

"No, it's just a made up character." *In a made up book.*

"Interesting," said Matt. "Where's it set?"

Arghh…

"Greece."

"Any particular part?"

"Not as yet. I'll home in on a location once I'm more into it."

That is, when I've looked at a map.

"Why not set it somewhere you've visited?"

"Yes, good idea."

"So what part of Greece would that be?"

"Um… I've not been there yet."

"Interesting. Do you think there could be authors who spend so much time writing about what their made up characters do, that they might look up one day and realize they haven't done anything themselves?"

"I've never thought of it like that."

"Could that happen to you?"

"No, but… regarding my characters…"

"Are they sleeping together?"

"What? They've only just met?"

"What does that have to do with it?"

"They have standards."

"Alcohol and summertime can overcome most standards."

"They aren't drunk and they're sitting in the shade. And, seriously, they've just met."

"Are they attracted to each other?"

"Yes."

"Big time or small time?"

"Big time."

"So she's wanting him badly but is prevented by an outside force."

"Yes, an outside force like…" *a laptop screen* "…they work for rival firms."

"That's good. Unless you want them to start out

hating each other and then gradually come to see the good in the other? Or he could seem great but actually be the wrong guy. You know, he seems nice, but she doesn't know his dark side – yet."

"It's a rom-com. Do you know much about romance?"

"Not really. I mainly read sci-fi."

"Oh."

"Obviously, we get occasional elements of romance, so similar rules might apply. For example, in the last book I read, the seemingly wonderful woman he met in chapter two was trying to eject him through the air lock in chapter ten."

"Yes, well, my two are having a light salad by the pool and she's not sure what to wear later."

"Okay, well, it sounds fun. Unfortunately though, I have to go."

"Could we talk again? It helps me get the juices flowing. The creative juices."

"Right. Okay."

"We'll speak again then."

"Yes."

With the call ended, Laura returned to the counter in the café. She would throw herself into this single afternoon of helping Tracy. And then two more.

"Matt seems nice," she said.

"He's okay – for an older brother. No, just kidding. He's a good guy."

"Is there a big age difference?"

"Five years. So I'm not exactly a spring chicken. Seriously though, I think Matt's been on his own too long. He's turning into Mr Boring."

"Oh?"

"Just as well he's on Planet Robbie for a week. That

must be shaking him out of it."

"Is he absolutely not the type to settle down?"

"He married young. Big mistake. They divorced when he was thirty. He's had a few near misses since, but I get the feeling he's thrown himself into his career now."

"Right."

Tracy laughed. "Unless he meets someone in Spain before Saturday."

Laura laughed too, but not on the inside.

16

An Idyll

#26: Sue Lyons

Posted 9 years ago

Hi, I remember the happy days of childhood holidays in Sandy Bay. It always seemed to be somewhere I'd like to live. Of course, once I was older, I appreciated how the summer view of the place isn't the real one. Most of the year it would just be a small, isolated village with very little happening. I'll probably go back there again though – in the summer, of course!

*

That evening, Laura and her family visited Shanklin Chine – a gorge of great natural beauty first opened to the public in 1817, making it the longest established attraction on the Isle of Wight. Like countless numbers before them, they took in its other-worldly tranquility as they made their way along the tree-lined chine that cuts its way from Shanklin Old Village to the beach below. Numerous artists, photographers and those seeking a spiritual moment had walked this way – from author Jane Austen to landscape painter J. M. W. Turner.

But while Laura took in the timeless beauty of the waterfall, the lush vegetation and towering trees, she couldn't quite forget the smile of a golf enthusiast in Alicante. She certainly fancied a romantic visit here with him at some point. Perhaps they would pause by the waterfall…?

And that's when she noticed a tear rolling down Bev's cheek.

"Are you okay, Mum?"

"Oh, I suppose it struck me I won't be coming here too many more times."

"Don't be silly. Of course you will."

"You will," Amy added. "Evie needs her great-gran."

They continued along the chine, strolling slowly, and Laura tried not to be too concerned. It was just a sentimental moment. That was all. Bev would be around for years to come yet.

"We've always had happy holidays," said Bev. "People have to rub along together, that's all. We've been doing it long enough."

"Yes, we have," said Laura.

"It must be a hundred years since we got started," said Bev. "Before my time, obviously. My grandad used to take a week in Eastbourne every September."

"You're beginning to sound like Harry," said Ross.

"Huh," said Harry. "Back then, my family couldn't afford a *day* in Eastbourne."

"Nor could ours for long," said Bev. "My grandad's firm went bust and the family struggled. After that, if you wanted a holiday away from home, you'd go hop-picking in Kent. That's how it was for me when I was young."

"It sounds like a different world," said Laura.

"What exactly was a hop-picking holiday?" asked Ross.

Bev explained with glowing fondness how poor, working class people went down to the countryside and picked the hops that made beer in exchange for a free stay in a makeshift cabin.

Ross looked puzzled.

"That's not really a holiday. It's more like a job. Did you pay tax?"

"Oh my God, Bev," Harry gasped. "You're under investigation. We'd better dig up your grandparents. They were the brains behind the operation."

"I was just asking out of curiosity," said Ross. "Just because you had a tax investigation thirty years ago doesn't mean you should hate all tax inspectors."

"What? I ended up paying more than most multinationals!"

"Honestly, Harry," said Bev, "it was only seven hundred."

"Exactly," said Harry. "More than most multinationals!"

"Let's change the subject," Laura ventured.

Ross walked off ahead to vape. Amy pushed Evie's buggy to catch up with him.

"Harry, be nice to him," said Bev. "He's doing his best."

"I *am* being nice to him."

Laura took her step-father aside like a naughty schoolboy.

"Harry, what is going on with you and Ross?" she asked once they were out of Bev's earshot.

"Nothing."

"Come on, spit it out."

"I told you – it's nothing."

"I'm still waiting, Harry."

"Okay, since you ask, I'm wondering if he's the right

man for Amy."

"Good grief – that is none of our business."

"He doesn't seem ready for fatherhood and I worry he'll poison things for Amy. For all of us."

"I hope you're not trying to drive him away?"

"Of course not. I just want the best for Amy. Honestly, we went to see them a couple of weeks ago, and… well, he ignored us. He ignored Amy and Evie, too. Amy got out some cake for tea and he went for a five-mile run."

"Perhaps they'd had an argument."

"So?"

"Perhaps he doesn't feel part of the family yet."

"When you join a family it doesn't come with guarantees of acceptance."

Laura winced a little. Harry was, after all, the man who came to take her dad's place in Bev's life.

"Okay," she said, "instead of confronting him, try a different tactic."

"Like what?"

"Use your brain. Share some of that wisdom of yours."

"I can hardly tell him how great fatherhood can be. I was never a father. And certainly not a good step-father to you. I could never break through that force field you put up."

"This isn't about us, it's about Amy and Ross."

"Yes, well… I'm sorry. When it comes to families, I can't help you. I spent most of my time with my uncle."

"Couldn't you use him as an example to share with Ross? You know, to show him how the wider family can get along?"

"Yes, possibly. He was certainly a good man."

"Maybe there's a little anecdote you could share."

"Yes… I suppose I could tell him how we used to go through the coastal towns in the 1950s. From May to September we'd sell stuff to the tourists. We'd start in Kent, then we'd work our way west – Sussex, Hampshire, Dorset, Devon… and we'd end up in Cornwall. Yes, he was a wonderful man. Someone you could trust."

"Yes… so why didn't you just stay in one town all summer?"

"Ah well, the stuff we sold was rubbish. We had to move on each day to avoid customers demanding a refund."

Laura sighed and tried to recapture the romance of the chine. Its beauty. Its timelessness. But it wasn't easy.

17

Getting Old

#27: David Trowbridge

Posted 9 years ago

I was at Hopton's Holiday Camp, Sandy Bay back in 1970. We went to the Isle of Wight Festival and saw Jimi Hendrix. The next day, we were back at Hopton's and the band playing in the ballroom was The Seaside Serenaders doing cheesy pop songs. It was like I'd been abducted by aliens and taken to a different planet. But no, I loved that place. So many good memories.

Freddie Archer replied 9 years ago

Hello everyone. Freddie here again. What a wonderful post, David. I worked at Hopton's at that time. I never made it to see Mr Hendrix, but I did enjoy the Seaside Serenaders. They used to finish with Those Were The Days, sung by a very talented orange coat called Georgie. Happy days!

*

It was half-ten on the Wednesday morning and Laura and her family were at the beach. With the temperature due to rise above 90 °F / 32 °C, they wanted to enjoy some time there before it turned into an oven. Laura was yet to mention the other reason for getting them there early, because it was too ludicrous to share. They would find out in time, of course. But, for now, she could relax. Or at least try.

"Everything okay?" she asked Amy, who was watching Ross play in the waves while Evie slept under the umbrella. "You seem like a quieter version of my daughter."

"I'm fine. Everything's going well and we have the wedding to look forward to."

Laura leaned in close for privacy. "I can hardly claim to be an expert, but I hope you two are on the same wavelength. If I learned anything from twenty years with your father, it's that it's too easy to drift off down your own path."

"I don't think that's going to happen to me and Ross. I agree with him that we should stick to our plan not to lose sight of the life we want."

"He seems to spend every weekend away doing triathlons or canoeing or something."

"That's his passion."

Laura could see that Amy was loyal to her man, even if he was somewhat more boy than man.

Just then, there was a minor commotion just along the beach. A young blond man with a scruffy hipster beard was with a woman who looked like a model. They seemed to have a photographer and a number of teenage girls following them.

"What the bloody hell's going on?" Harry protested.

"It's not thingy, is it?" said Amy.

"Thingy?" said Laura, wondering why their peace was being disturbed.

"It was the Isle of Wight festival last weekend. He must have stayed on for some R and R."

"Lucky him," said Laura.

"He's all over social media," said Amy, "but you won't believe I haven't listened to any of his music. I'm so over the hill."

"You're only twenty-seven," said Laura.

"Exactly. That guy's twenty. His fans are fourteen. I'm ancient."

Laura studied the bearded scruff. He looked like he'd been stranded on a desert island for the past year.

"Maybe he should change his image?" said Bev.

"Yeah," said Harry, "his current image looks like a mattress exploded in his face."

"We mustn't get too judgmental about young people," said Amy.

Laura was wide-eyed. Then she supposed this was Harry's conveyor belt of life in motion. The bloody thing never seemed to stop. Now Amy, at *twenty-seven*, would soon be extolling her own version of the good old days.

"Just think," said Harry. "That guy could be a star for the next fifty years. Imagine that. Still, it could provide employment for look-a-likes."

"What a thought," said Laura.

"It's a good business," said Harry. "I used to know a bloke who looked like Benny Hill. He used to have people come up to him and he'd have to walk away, usually quite fast, while they hummed the speeded up tune from the show."

"This is a joke, right?" said Amy.

"It's no joke. Charlie Beale, his name was, and he was the dead image of Benny Hill."

"He must have been sick to death of it," said Laura.

"What? You must be kidding. He quit his job as a dock worker, signed on with an agency, and made a fortune."

Over the next hour or so, the pop star moved on, Ross returned and the family settled down to some peace and quiet. Then, just before half-twelve, Laura got up from under her umbrella.

"We could probably do with getting some lunch," said Bev.

"I fancy a frappe-latte and corned beef hash," said Ross.

Harry tutted. "We used to have corned beef when I was a kid. Mind you, we were so poor our corned beef was made from old tea leaves and soap."

"That's not true," said Ross.

"And," Harry went on, "if you wanted weird coffee, you'd take it without milk."

Amy stepped in. "Ross, Harry, let's not argue all the time."

"All I said was I fancy a frappe-latte and corned beef hash," said Ross, "and Harry starts up again about how he was poorer than everyone else."

"No, I don't."

"Yes, you do. Next you'll be saying how you had to wear a school uniform made of cardboard and eat sandwiches filled with old newspaper."

Laura insisted. "Ross, Harry — try to be less argumentative."

"I'm old," said Harry, "I have less and less time to share my thoughts."

Laura sighed. "It's not like the family holidays we had when I was little."

Bev baulked. "What are you talking about? It's *exactly* like the holidays we had when you were little. Your gran used to argue with your dad all the time. Those home movies were filmed when the sun came out, when we were having fun. Ross and Amy's Instagram photos are the same."

"You're probably right," said Laura, getting her stuff together. "Anyway, you'll laugh when I tell you this, but I'm pretending to be a local."

There was no laughter. Just bemusement.

"How do you mean?" said Amy.

"I told a woman in Fore Street I'm a local."

"A local?" Bev and Ross echoed.

"Yes, from East Cowes."

"Is it the heat?" said Harry. "Has it got to you?"

"It's not the heat," Laura reassured him.

"The menopause?" Harry offered.

"No, it's not the bloody menopause. I've taken a part-time job."

Ross's brow furrowed. "While pretending to be a local from East Cowes?"

"Yes."

"And would this job involve dressing in catering gear so you can work in a souvenir shop?"

"Not quite."

"Laura...?" said Bev, seemingly in need of further information, but equally unable to find the words.

"I said we should all be free to do separate things," said Laura. "That was always part of the plan for this holiday."

"Are you *sure* it's not the heat?" Harry enquired again. "You hear of people going crazy in the Sahara."

"No, it's not the heat, or the menopause, or dengue flippin' fever," said Laura. "Seriously, I have to go to work."

And with that, she strode away in the direction of Fore Street.

18

This Woman's Work

#28: Mr Phillip Whyte

Posted 8 years ago

We were at Sandy Bay recently. It has a Blue Flag beach – that's an award for being clean to an outstanding level. What I learned by a chance conversation is how much work volunteers do without any Government funding to earn that flag. During the summer, they go out in boats and work the water, removing trash. They also go over the beach with rakes and sacks daily at seven a.m. Not many people get to see that. Good work, Sandy Bay.

Freddie Archer replied 8 years ago

Hello everyone. Freddie here again. What a wonderful thing to read. Good work indeed, Sandy Bay! I really must return there one day. It's been too long.

*

Laura arrived at the half full Moorings café determined to cut her time working there as short as possible. She still couldn't get her fling with Matt right in her head. After all, it wasn't technically a fling, or any kind of holiday romance. It was just two people talking about stuff over the internet.

"Hi Tess," she called to her co-worker.

"You ever tried Trance Yoga?" asked Tess. She was clearing a table by the window.

"No, I can't say I have."

"Don't. It's a killer."

"I can imagine."

She looked around for Tracy without luck, so she headed for the business side of the counter, where Tess came to join her.

"When I told my daughter I was going to a specialist yoga class, well… the surprise on her face." Tess lowered her voice. "You'd think I'd said I was dating her boyfriend."

Laura cringed.

"So it's a keep fit thing then?" she managed to ask.

"Yes, I was curious to see where I stood on the fitness scale. You know, between Olympic athlete and dead body."

"And?"

"Don't ask. Seriously, when the instructor said 'on your knees, please' I got down on my knees and continued straight down onto my face."

A couple of customers came in. Laura began to serve them.

"I do need to get fit though," said Tess. "I don't mean fit-fit, I mean fit enough to attempt getting fit."

But Laura got stuck into her work and wasn't able to answer.

Eventually Tracy came down from upstairs followed by Liz and Bonzo.

"Hi Laura," she said. "Janet's not well."

"Oh crap."

"It's okay," said Liz. "Me and Bonzo should be alright. We'll call out if we need help."

Laura knew she couldn't abandon them just yet.

"No problem, Liz. I'll be here."

A young couple Laura had just handed a ticket to went out the back to grab a table.

Liz whispered.

"Orange coats from the camp. Off duty."

"Ah," Laura whispered back. "They certainly work hard."

It drew a reaction from Liz.

"I nearly married an orange coat back in the sixties."

"Oh?"

"Ancient history, Laura. We were engaged for a while, but…"

Liz turned and headed for the door into the souvenir side of the empire.

Just then, Laura's phone rang. It was Amy.

Oh my God…

Laura answered it, stepping out into the street as she did so.

"Amy? Is everything okay?"

"Nothing to worry about, Mum. Thing is, I'm not sure where to draw the line with Ross. I agreed with him at the start, but…"

"But you don't now?"

"Yes. I mean no, I don't."

"Right, so you don't agree with him about what?"

"Would you agree that motherhood is an incredibly strong bond?"

"I think that goes without saying."

"And would you say that fatherhood is an incredibly strong bond?"

"Ah."

"Because I'm beginning to think fatherhood might be a chore."

"Well… it might not be that."

"Oh?"

Laura found she'd left Fore Street and was facing the view of the estuary. Some people were having a great time taking holiday photos by the boats alongside the nearest jetty.

"Well, it might be that, Amy, but, for some men bonding can take longer. They tend to stand back a little because they can see the mother and baby bond is so strong. They can feel a bit like they're trespassing."

"Is that what you think Ross feels?"

"I have no idea what he feels, and I'm certainly no expert. It might be true though, and it might explain why he's keener than ever on doing more and more activities. He'll change though. In time. He'll see it's the right path for him too."

"Harry chips away at him, doesn't he. Do you think he sees that Ross isn't a good enough dad?"

"I'm sure Harry doesn't see it like that at all. I think he's just keen to get Ross to focus on… well, Harry had a terrible childhood."

"Yes, I know… he sometimes says how his dad never did anything with him."

"Maybe Harry doesn't want that happening to Evie."

"Yes, I suppose… okay, Mum. Thanks."

"Right, well, I'll see you later. We can talk more if you want."

"Yes, I'd like that."

*

After the lunch rush, there was something of a respite before the cream teas got going. Laura was with Tess, tidying up the deserted outdoor area.

"It's not bad work," said Tess. "I'll have to see going forward though. I've tried to get an office job. I quite fancy doing admin."

"No luck?"

"No responses. I put myself out there to twenty companies and the offers came flooding in... in my dreams."

"Oh well."

"Actually, I did get one response. They asked me to complete a personal questionnaire as honestly as possible, which was basically asking me to self-assassinate."

"Oh well, keep trying. You never know."

"To be honest, I think I look completely stagnated on my CV. They probably think I died ten years ago. I'm surprised they haven't sent the police round to remove my corpse."

"Finding the right job is never easy. I've... tried. My last boss, Angela. What a demon. It was endless emails, all day, all night, all weekend."

"I always find a well-placed eff off usually does the trick. Still, there will always be those who put up with it. Weak women, usually. So sad to see that. We have to be strong. Get the right partner and the right job. It's not too much to ask, is it?"

"No... it's not."

Laura thought about filling some cream and jam pots, but another idea popped into her head. If she couldn't sort out Angela...

She found Tracy at the counter.

"I don't suppose Matt might be free for a minute?"

"I'll text him," said Tracy.

Laura attended to the cream and jam, all the while waiting for her boss to give her the nod.

It came five minutes later.

"I'll get the laptop out," said Tracy.

"No need," said Laura. "I'll connect on my phone. Could you text him to accept my request?"

Tracy smiled. "Will do."

Three minutes later, Laura was down by the boats on the estuary.

A face appeared on her phone.

"Hi Matt. I realized I never said goodbye."

"Okay…"

"Okay, so before I do, in my novel… does he love 'em and leave 'em?"

"I'm not sure. What do you think?"

"I don't think he does."

"You don't? Okay, I suppose it depends if you want him to be a bad guy who needs taming. Then, he could be a love 'em and leave 'em kind of guy until he meets this particular woman. Then he's torn about it. Or you could write him as a total bad boy. Millions of books are sold with a bad boy on the cover. He's usually exposing his chest – oh, a bit like me. Hang on, I'll find a T-shirt."

"No, it's okay. You were saying?"

"Oh… well, a lot of people enjoy reading about a bad boy. In a book, they can get up close and personal with someone they probably wouldn't encounter in real life. It's good escapism, which is healthy. Unless we allow it to take over."

"Yes, I agree. It's important to know where the line is. That side of the line, healthy. This side, unhealthy."

"You mean this side healthy, that side, unhealthy."

"Yes, that's what I meant. Do you think they could be soul mates?"

"Okay, that's a bit out of the blue. So… yes. I'm going to sound very unscientific, but I believe there's a soul in all of us, a consciousness that science cannot fully explain. I believe we're one with the universe. In fact I believe our hearts and minds could be the universe brought to life through a single focus in order to understand itself."

"Sorry, is this you speaking or my character?"

"Pardon?"

"It's you, obviously. Sorry. That's very profound."

"If you want profound, wait till I get started on Southampton Football Club. There I can go to whole new depths of meaning."

"I quite like football."

"Maybe we'll bump into each other one day at a game."

"That would be nice."

There was a pause.

"Carl Jung said something interesting," said Matt. "The meeting of two personalities is like the contact of two chemical substances – if there's any reaction, both are transformed."

"I'll keep that in mind. For my characters, I mean."

"Right, well…"

"Are you on holiday to meet women?"

"Pardon?"

"Tracy says your friend Robbie booked the trip so he could meet lots of women who are keen to… well… share his view of the world."

"I'm sure Tracy told you how I'm trying my best to keep this a healthy, fun trip we guys we will remember for all the right reasons. I'm doing well so far – and we fly home Saturday morning."

"Yes, just to be clear, what do you consider the right reasons?"

"You sound worried."

"I'm not. I'm just using my experience to say don't do anything you'll regret."

"You have experience of that kind of holiday?"

"No, I…"

"It's a golf holiday, Laura. That's all. I've moved on from worrying about women. I'm the complete opposite of my younger self. Back then, I used to imagine the love of my life arriving with every new batch of tourists. Innocent kid stuff."

"But then, like that Bible quote, 'When you became a man you put away childish things'…"

"I don't think that's a Bible quote. I think it's C. S. Lewis."

Ooh, C. S. Lewis – good accidental quote.

"Yes, well, C. S. Lewis meant he was all grown up by then."

"Well, no – the Bible quote makes that point. 'When I was a child, I spoke like a child, I thought like a child, I reasoned like a child. When I became a man, I gave up childish ways.' It's from Corinthians, I think."

"Right."

"I think C. S. Lewis was saying something different. 'When I became a man I put away childish things, including the fear of childishness.' Hang on, I'll just flip you off the screen a sec… yep, I've got it… 'When I was ten, I read fairy tales in secret and would have been ashamed if I had been found doing so. Now that I am fifty, I read them openly. When I became a man I put away childish things, including the fear of childishness and the desire to be very grown up.' Okay, you're back on my screen now. Do you know, Laura, this is the first interesting conversation I've had today. Robbie just asked me if his shorts looked too tight."

"Well, er… are you a fan of C. S. Lewis?"

"A little, perhaps."

"I've read The Lion, The Witch and the Wardrobe. At least, I did forty years ago."

"Interesting series of books. J. R. R. Tolkien mocked Lewis for their lack of symbolism, and yet Lewis never told him how each book is laden with it. Based on the old map of the heavens, no less."

"How interesting."

"Really? It bores most people witless. Still, you're a novelist."

Oh yes – I'd forgotten that.

"Well, listen to us, discussing literature…"

Laura's phone pinged. It was an email from Angela.

"Well, I'd better be going," said Matt. "Nice to talk to you."

"Oh right. Nice to talk to you too."

With the call over, Laura returned to the café, where a customer was waiting.

Ah, the cheese and pickle lady.

"Hi there. How are you?"

"Oh fine, thank you, Laura."

"Did you manage to get to Osborne House?"

"Yes, the bus dropped me right outside. It was a lovely morning."

"Great. So, um… what can I get you?"

"A pot of tea and a slice of apple pie, please."

"Would you like cream with the pie?"

"No… yes. Yes, please. And I'll sit outside."

Before Laura could move a muscle, her phone rang.

"Hi Angela, I'm a bit busy."

"It's just the fleshing out of a course. You'll be delivering it, so I'll leave it in your capable hands. I attached it to the email I sent for convenience. Did you get it?"

"Yes, I got it, thanks."

"Teachers need to be engaged when delivering relationship education. It's our job to see they are brimful of confidence in the way they deliver that information."

"Yes, I know that, Angela."

"This course will guide schools in understanding the requirements for each phase. We're talking about the school's duty to cultivate student wellbeing, good decision making, and resilience."

An elderly couple came in. They looked like they'd been married forever.

Laura smiled at them.

"It's a fast-changing social media world, Laura, and young people are struggling when boundaries are pushed."

"Is your jam raspberry or strawberry?" the man asked.

"Trained teachers and mentors play a vital role in guiding students away from negative environments to a place of positivity, self-confidence, opportunity, and success."

"Strawberry," she whispered.

"The future wellbeing of the next generation is in our hands."

"Only the raspberry bits stick in our teeth."

"It's a biggie, Laura."

"It's definitely strawberry."

"Two cream teas then, please," said the man, offering a debit card.

"Righto… yes, why not create two distinct courses. One for senior management and one for teachers on the front line. We could do both on the same day. Any thoughts, Angela?"

"I'll get back to you."

"If you could tap your card just there, please."

19

Progress

#29: raceboyrogers

Posted 8 years ago

I worked at Sandy Bay 1977 to 79 and lived on camp. What great times! I remember Ralph the Head Orange Coat, who had been there forever, and Lenny who became a multiplex cinema manager in the Midlands. I bumped into Ralph in 2000. He was an entertainer with a small independent camp in Devon, doing his 'naughty headmaster' routine and saucy lyrics to well-known songs, which seemed less funny to me as he was way over 70 by then. He said he feared retirement. I bet he's still working now, poor guy.

*

Approaching Chalet 44 after work, Laura was wondering what to tell her family about her job at the café. It seemed completely ridiculous to be working during a holiday trip on which she was meant to be relaxing, but…

Activity outside Chalet 45 caught her eye. The teen girl was talking quietly with a teen boy. Her mother came out and the boy departed. Laura could read the situation like a book. A book she'd lived. In fact, that exact chapter.

Bev waved. Laura waved back and beheld her family on the shady part of the patio.

Evie – asleep in a baby nest with a slight breeze ruffling the little flags tied to the chair beside her.

Amy – taking a well-earned chance to doze on a sunbed alongside.

Bev – looking up from her women's magazine.

Harry – reading a spy novel.

Ross – checking his phone.

They were precious. Some more than others, perhaps. Bev, Amy, and Evie were everything to her. Was that sexist? Why were the men lower down the list?

No, it was just… how it was. The men were originally outsiders, that was all. The main thing was them all sharing their time together. Well, most of it. The trouble was that they didn't hear much from the real Laura – the one who had never stopped dreaming about a more fulfilling future. To them, the life she had today looked perfectly fine. A woman with a nice home, a good job, and a loving family. Who could want for more?

Harry looked up from his book.

"Everything alright?"

"Yes, all good, thanks. How's your novel?"

"Terrible. I could write something better tied to a typewriter falling off a cliff."

"I'm sure it's harder than that. I've been trying myself."

"What, to write a novel?"

Now Ross joined Bev and Harry in staring at Laura.

"Well, I've got the basic idea mapped out."

"Since when have you been doing that?" said Ross.

"Over the past few days."

"Wow," said Harry. "First she gets a job, now she's writing a novel. It doesn't say much for our company."

"Don't be silly."

"Me?"

"Where's it set?" asked Bev.

"Greece."

"Oh great," complained Ross.

"Well, I couldn't set it on the Isle of Wight."

"I said months ago we should go to Greece," said Ross in an appeal to Bev. "Now Laura's bored of the Isle of Wight and she's gone there without us."

"Only in her head," said Harry.

"I'll put the kettle on," said Laura, disappearing inside.

A few minutes later, they were enjoying tea and cake outside.

"Anyone know much about C. S. Lewis?" Laura asked.

"I'll google it," said Ross.

"No need," said Harry. "I've read the Chronicles of Narnia. All seven books."

"Have you?" said Laura. "What did you make of it?"

"It's got a lot of Christian stuff in it. Then there's the Greek and Roman stuff – mythology, I mean. And there's British and Irish folklore. Oh, and some bloke found a whole new hidden layer of meaning in there too."

"You mean the heavenly bodies," said Laura, quoting Matt.

"You know about that? You're not as dim as you look."

"Thanks Harry. You really must cut down on the compliments."

"Just kidding. Yeah, he wrote a load of medieval cosmology into the series and nobody knew. So each book is actually based on the Sun, the Moon, Mars, Mercury, Venus, Jupiter and Saturn."

"You like Lewis then?"

"Not really. I just wanted to get one over on Dennis McCarthy. He was always bragging about what books he'd read, so, when I turned sixty, I decided to read as many as I could."

"That's impressive."

"Not really. He's dead now so I can't brag back at him. He was a good friend though. We used to watch football together."

A ball came over. All eyes turned to the five-year-old boy from Chalet 43.

"Hey, Ross," said Harry. "Give that kid a moment of your time. Childhood is short and it's not always great. Go over there and make his minute."

"His minute?"

"Well, you're not likely to make his day, so use your own advice and start small."

Ross shrugged, got up, and kicked the ball back. Then he sat down again.

"Thanks," said the boy.

Harry raised his eyes to the heavens and sighed.

*

As a prelude to dinner, the family went for a walk, following a public footpath that led from the holiday park's front gate away to a hill that overlooked the estuary. Halfway to the top, a road cut across the path. Here, an ancient signpost pointed the ways to Sandy Bay and Newport. Laura knew the spot well. There were photos spanning the decades of various family members standing against that signpost – none more cherished than the photo sequences that showed younger members growing from toddler to teen.

"During the War, they removed all the signs," said Harry. "It was in case Nazi Germany invaded. If you got lost, you really got lost."

"Didn't they just turn them to face the wrong way?" said Bev.

"That was in comedy films," said Harry.

"Photo time," said Laura. "Stand against the signpost, everyone. If we do it every few years, we'll capture Evie growing taller."

"Yeah," said Harry, "and you'll capture me growing shorter."

They took turns taking photos and posing, and then Ross produced a selfie stick to get them all in.

Back on the upward path, Harry walked beside Laura.

"So what's your book about?" he asked.

"If I write it... it'll be a romance."

"Soppy or hot?"

"Well, not explicit, obviously, but—"

"What do you mean, 'obviously'?"

"I'm a mother. No, cancel that. I'm a grandmother."

Harry chuckled, not unkindly. "So this tame love story...?"

"It won't be tame. It'll be full of passion. They just won't... you know."

"They will," insisted Harry. "They'll just wait till you're not there. You can't change the way the world works."

"It's a story about hope... and heart... and putting things right. There's this guy..."

"In the book or in real life?"

"What?"

"The way your cheeks are flushing, I'm thinking he's real."

"Yes, well, there *is* a guy."

Laura was suddenly aware of her entire family peering

at her. And, if she wasn't mistaken, two young women ten feet away pretending to read a map.

"Who is he, Laura?" said Bev, looking concerned.

Laura waited for the map readers to move on.

"I think I've met the right man for me."

"Seriously?" said Amy.

"It's not a holiday romance thing, is it?" said Harry.

"No. Well, yes. Kind of."

"Where's he staying?" said Bev.

"In Spain."

"Spain?" said her entire family in unison.

"Yes, he's on holiday in Spain," said Laura, matter-of-factly.

"How do you... meet up with him?" Harry asked.

"On a laptop."

"Oh Laura," Bev gasped. "You're not paying him?"

Tears seemed to be welling up in her eyes.

"Of course not. It's a perfectly straightforward holiday romance... kind of thing."

Ross chimed in. "Let me get this straight. While on a break in England, you're having a holiday fling with a man in Spain?"

"Hold on, Ross," said Harry. "She doesn't need advice from a man who sits on an English beach listening to bird noises from Brazil."

"So who is this man in Spain?" asked Amy.

"Good question," said Ross. "He could be one of those scammers who steals money from your account. Have you checked your account recently?"

"I wish I hadn't mentioned him now," said Laura.

Bev shook her head. "If a relationship has to hidden away, it's the wrong relationship."

"Bev's right," said Harry. "You'll never be happy operating in the shadows."

"What is this?" Laura protested. "Have you two started an advice blog?"

"What would we know?" said Harry. "We've only got a hundred and sixty years of experience between us."

"A hundred and fifty nine," said Bev, correcting him.

"So, basically," said Ross, "it's a holiday romance with a man on a different vacation."

Harry turned to Bev. "At least she can't get pregnant."

"Okay, so my life isn't perfect," said Laura. "Breaking news, guys, it hasn't been for years."

"Okay, so the man in the novel is real," said Harry. "But he's in Spain? Only you said he was in Greece."

"Don't confuse things," said Laura. "I'm not writing a novel. I just told the man in Spain I was, and that it was set in Greece. I've not done internet dating before, to be honest."

"Well, that's okay," said Bev. "If it's a holiday romance, he obviously has some feelings for you."

"Well, no," said Laura, "I haven't led *him* to believe it's a holiday romance."

"You haven't?"

"No."

"But you'd like it to be," said Amy.

"Well, yes. I'm not made of stone."

"So what's keeping this one-sided romance alive?"

"The novel."

"The novel that doesn't exist?"

"Yes."

Bev's brow furrowed. "So, your one-sided romance is based on you writing a novel…"

"…a fictional novel," said Harry. "It doesn't exist."

Bev tried again. "So you're pretending to write a novel about a woman having a holiday romance in Greece, so you can impress a man on holiday in Spain who you're not having a romance with because you're in England?"

"It sounds simple when you put it like that," said Harry.

"So when did you meet this man?" Bev asked.

"Forty years ago."

"Now it sounds even simpler," said Harry.

Laura sighed. "Do you think the sun's affecting my judgement?"

They walked on, higher up the hill as Laura explained about the boy from the café all those years ago.

Near the top, Ross's phone pinged.

"Ah… here's something," he said, checking it with glee. "There's a guy who does sky-diving. He was all booked up but I asked him to let me know if he had anyone cancel on him. Harry – how about you and I go up?"

There was a collective female gasp.

"What's all the gasping for?" said Harry. "I did part of my National Service with the paratroopers."

"That was sixty years ago!" Bev blasted. "You can't go up there now."

Laura tried to make sense of it. "Ross, you can't throw Harry out of a plane – however tempting that might be."

"He can jump with a guide," said Ross.

"I don't need a guide," said Harry. "I've jumped out of more planes than you've had hot dinners."

Bev intervened. "Harry can't jump out of a plane. He can sit and he can walk, but he mustn't ride a bike or a horse, and so I'm fairly certain parachuting is out too."

"You're exaggerating," said Harry.

But Bev seemed determined to protect him from himself.

"Harry, you've had treatment. You can't take part."

"Well, thank you for sharing my private life with half

the island," said Harry.

Laura went to put her arm around him, but he dodged her embrace and went off.

All fell silent.

"Let's get to the top," said Bev, peering up to the modest peak. "I'd like to see the view."

She set off.

Laura joined her.

"Is everything alright, Mum?"

"When you're struggling, just take a small next step."

"Do you mean the hill or Harry's health?"

"No, I mean you with your new man."

"Oh. Right."

Laura wondered. And then decided to ignore Bev's advice.

She'd taken enough small steps in life.

It was time to take a giant one.

20

Full Steam Ahead

#30: DorsetJimmyTownsend

Posted 8 years ago

I went to Hopton's, Sandy Bay with my parents in the 80s. I was 18 and didn't really want to go as my mates were going to Cyprus (I couldn't afford it). I dragged my feet following Mum and Dad around for the first few days. Then I met a girl in the ballroom. Debs was just a few months younger than me and in the same unfortunate dire financial straits. We soon worked out a plan to go and do stuff together that was relatively low cost. We kidded ourselves for a while that our only focus was on getting something out of a disastrous fortnight, but it gradually became clear that we had no intention of ever parting regardless of her living 130 miles away from me. I know it sounds corny, but our holiday romance was the real thing. Now after being in love with Debs for 35 years (and married for 33) I am eternally grateful to my wonderful (and still sprightly!) parents for dragging a stroppy, reluctant teen to the Isle of Wight all those years ago!

Freddie Archer replied 8 years ago

Hello everyone. Freddie here. What a wonderful story, Jimmy. Good ol' parents for getting you to Sandy Bay! Fate is certainly a magical force.

*

It was just after eight on Thursday morning. Laura had been up since six, working at the chalet's dining table – at least, trying to work. Her efforts were continually interrupted by the same thought – six of their ten nights in Sandy Bay had gone.

For the umpteenth time, she refocused on a plan for helping teachers who were responsible for delivering relationship guidance to their teenage students. As usual, Laura's aim wasn't just on what these teachers would impart, but how they would impart it. In short, how, in a classroom, they might deal with sensitive relationship issues without creating an atmosphere of awkwardness and embarrassment.

Being sensible. That was the way. The school wasn't there to replace the life lessons awaiting young teens, merely to offer guidance as to potential trigger points in any relationship journey. Creating a common sense process was the way. Focus on the journey in terms of what benefits smart thinking would bring.

Laura made notes identifying the key steps from Acquaintance to Full Relationship, suggesting that students were guided to always stop before each step and ask themselves 'Is this what I want right now?', 'Am I doing this solely to ease social pressure?'... The approach would help the teacher keep a strong focus on the subject of How To Control Your Relationship Journey.

But what if she was overlooking something? What if the key steps weren't quite so obviously separate to every young person? What if 'heat of the moment' blurred their ability to assess and appraise?

She found some feedback from last year. A teacher in Manchester referred to a thirteen-year-old girl asking 'How will I know for sure if I love someone?'

Laura sat back.

Good question.

*

Two hours later, Laura and her family were on the platform at Haven Street, one of four stations on the Isle of Wight Steam Railway. Laura loved the nostalgic feel of this heritage line, with every detail taking them back a century.

"What a sight," said a man nearby, referring to Calbourne the tank engine pulling its train into the station with lots of steam and noise for the benefit of the many tourists waiting to board it.

Laura turned to smile at Bev, but she was standing back looking a little tearful.

"Are you okay, Mum?"

"I was just seeing you standing there when you were two years old. We were waiting for a train just like this one. Mandy was with me, you were with your dad, holding his hand tight. Fifty years ago, that was. How can that much time have passed?"

"That's a nice memory, Mum. I didn't know they had a heritage rail line back then."

"Now I think of it, it wasn't a heritage line back then.

It was probably just a diesel engine pulling old carriages. They were getting rid of steam around that time. Your dad never approved. He said there was romance in steam. He was right, of course. There *was* romance in steam. And soot too. You'd get it in your hair – like we are now. He always saw the positive side of things. Always."

The train came to a halt. They were directly in front of a carriage door.

Laura leaned in close. "Do you miss him?"

"I'm alright, love. I've got Harry."

"I know, but do you miss him? Do you miss Jim Cass?"

Bev sighed and opened the door.

"There's not a day goes by that I don't miss that man. Not a single day."

Along with Ross, Amy, Evie and Harry, they boarded the train and took their seats.

Laura wasn't sure if the carriages were Victorian or Edwardian, but they had been beautifully restored. She thought of sitting on a train all those years ago alongside her beloved dad. Time seemed so fleeting. What you had, you couldn't hold on to forever – and sometimes not for very long at all.

Then she thought of Matt. What stations lay ahead on their line? What was their ultimate destination?

The shrill sound of a guard's whistle was followed swiftly by the chugging of the steam engine. But as the train began to pull out of the station, Laura felt she was on a different journey.

*

At Smallbrook Junction, they got off and had a brief look around. Then it was a short wait for a train to take them back through Ashey and Haven Street, and on to the other end of the line at Wootton – from where they would finally come back again to Haven Street.

Bev had wandered over to an old bench where Ross, Amy and Evie were seated. She was soon turning it into a photo opportunity.

"This takes me back," said Harry.

"Steam?"

"Yes, we lived near a railway. I used to watch the trains and get a sense that some kind of freedom was waiting for me, if only I could afford the price of a ticket. I used to imagine going to all kinds of places. Cornwall, Scotland…"

"I'd imagine every child dreams of something."

"The Flying Scotsman," said Harry. "You've heard of it?"

"Of course. It's our most famous steam train."

"Steam *engine*. The train's the thing it pulls."

"Yes, of course."

"I'm glad I came on this holiday," said Harry. "I wasn't sure, but now I'm pleased."

"I didn't realize you had doubts," said Laura.

"Well, you're busy at work and we don't have that much of a relationship."

"That's a bit harsh, Harry."

Harry lowered his voice. "I wouldn't want to be old and on my own waiting for you to visit, Laura. You're a lovely woman, but let's agree we wouldn't see much of each other, if at all."

Laura didn't like that.

"I'd make the effort," she assured him.

"Ah duty," said Harry. "Did I ever tell you about the Monday Club? It's a place for elderly people to go once a week. You know, to get out of the house."

"And you find it helps you?"

"I'm not an attendee! I'm a bloody volunteer!"

"Ah, sorry."

There was a pause while Harry calmed down.

"There are several people there, in their eighties and nineties, who receive no visitors to their homes," he explained. "That's a big fat zero, every day of every week."

"It's quite a thing these days. You see stories on the news about it."

"In many cases, it's circumstances. The poor old soul never had much chance due to other people dying and so on. But there are those who had opportunities to do something and failed."

"How do you mean?"

"Arnold."

"Arnold?"

"He's a Monday Club regular. Do you know he always gets a birthday card, Father's Day card and Christmas card from his daughter?"

"Well, that's something."

"And one visit per year, in the summer, so they can sit outside in his little garden."

"What are you saying, Harry?"

"Me and Bev think this holiday is a great opportunity to put this family right. Well, Bev thinks it and I agree."

"Mum has done more than enough."

"No, we mean it's a great opportunity for you."

"Me?"

"Yes, you. It's a bit late in the day for us. We're on the great conveyor belt of life, remember? It's always moving. When Evie was placed on it, Amy moved along from daughter to mother, you went from mother to gran, and Bev and me... well, we'll soon be falling off the end."

"That's a bit dramatic, Harry."

"It's life. Plain and simple. But there's something I was thinking about last night in bed. It explains why Arnold hardly ever sees his daughter even though they're family."

"And the answer is…?"

"He overlooked friendship."

"Oh?"

"That's it. He's relied on duty and look where it's got him."

"What makes you think I'm not friends with Amy?"

"Oh dear, you really don't get it, do you."

"Get what? You're not making sense. As usual."

Harry looked over to Bev and the others, but they had moved farther down the platform to have photos taken in front of the station sign.

"Okay, here's how it works," said Harry. "First you have to hug two men."

"What?"

"Three if you get a date with the man in Spain."

"What are you talking about?"

"I've checked it with Bev. This is solid stuff. You just have to create a moment… where the only logical thing to do… is hug Ross and me."

"What?"

"It doesn't have to be at the same time. In fact, it probably can't be. Anyway, I've made some discreet enquiries and you haven't had close contact with a man in decades."

"Harry…"

"Being friends is what makes a family work. You've already got the duty part, but it won't make the family a success if you only ever pull that lever."

"I am friends."

"Not with me or Ross."

"That's…"

"That's why getting the whole clan together for a week or two is important for some families. This family being one of them. Bev understands that. Mind you, it can't just be about splashing in the waves and entering the knobbly knees competition. It has to be about the different generations becoming actual, real friends. We don't think this family is quite there and we're worried."

"About me?"

"Yes, you remind me of Arnold. When he was younger, he worked and made some money, but that was it."

"Are you saying he never made friends with his daughter?"

"No, I'm saying he never made friends with his daughter's husband. And now he relies on duty."

"I'm having a holiday with Amy and Ross."

"Didn't Bev push you into that?"

"That's… okay, that's true."

"Ross wanted to go to Greece without you."

"I know. But that's their choice and I respect that. I'd never interfere."

"I'm not saying you'll end up like Arnold, I'm just saying you're in danger of not being friends with Ross and that means you'll be relying on duty rather than friendship."

"They don't live far. I can always see them."

"Ross wants to live on the south coast. That'll be at least a hundred miles from you. And Amy agrees."

Laura was shocked.

"How do you know?"

"Amy told Bev yesterday. Ross wants to set up his own business as a tax consultant."

"Amy told my mum?"

"Yes, they're friends."

"Why hasn't anyone told me?"

"I just did – because I think we could become friends."

Laura suddenly felt strangely separate and alone.

"I've been getting it wrong," said Harry. "I was worried Ross was the wrong man, but I wasn't taking into account Amy's determination to make it work. She gets that from you."

"I would never stand in their way. Never."

"I know."

"So that's why you think this holiday is an opportunity… for me."

"I think it's your only opportunity."

"I didn't realize…"

"Work with me, Laura. We need to make sure Ross and Amy are okay as a couple. They're not at the moment."

"Right…"

"First, we need to make you friends with both of them, because then they'll buy a house on the coast that has a spare room for you to stay in. Then you'll never be Arnold."

"This all seems very unreal."

"Making friends with your family will be a joy. You just have to find time to work at it. Only it's Thursday and we go home on Monday. Then you'll be back at work."

Laura sighed. "I thought my mission was to have ten days of calm."

"No, your mission is to save this family from drifting apart."

"Yes, I can see that now. Thanks Harry. You're rude and you poke your nose into other people's business, but thank you."

"It could be time for that hug."

"I think you're right."

They hugged. Harry smelled nice, but Laura was shocked at how bony he was.

"I'm sorry we've been distant," she said as they pulled apart. There was a little tear in the corner of her eye.

"I was never going to replace your dad," said Harry. "And it was never my aim to even try. I only wanted to support you. So on that score, at least I seem to be getting somewhere."

"Harry, you will never become an Arnold."

"Thank God for that."

"I owe you. That's the biggest slap in the face I've had since Jonathan walked out. Only this one I deserved. And I appreciate it."

"Let's catch up with the others," said Harry. "Looks like our train's coming in."

21

A Room With A View

#31: Ron Goodman

Posted 8 years ago

My holiday memories are really special to me. We went to many camps during the 60s and early 70s but Hopton's Sandy Bay was the best. We went six times and we always took my nan. An earlier post mentions a steelworker dad – well, it was the same with Nan. She was this slow, tired old lady, let down by a disappearing husband and let down by life, too, really. She was always trudging back from the shops or the market with heavy bags and a frown. But for two weeks every year, she dropped 30 years and became this laughing, daft lovable nan who did everything with us kids, from paddling in the sea to singing 'the sun has got his hat on' to dancing with us in the ballroom. Thanks Sandy Bay. You gave me the best of my nan and I'll never forget that.

Freddie Archer replied 8 years ago

Hello everyone. Freddie here. That's a lovely story, Ron. God bless your nan!

Bonnie Sawyer replied 8 years ago

Lovely comments, Ron. I used to go to Hopton's at Sandy Bay too. It was Gran and Grandad, my mum and dad, me and my brother and sisters, plus aunts, uncles and cousins. We had such a laugh. Great times! Forty years on, I'm good friends with my cousins and I put that down to our big family holidays together.

Freddie Archer replied 8 years ago

That's lovely to hear, Bonnie. And so true. The power of having fun together when you're young really does make for stronger bonds in later life.

*

Laura arrived at the Moorings café just before half-twelve. This would be her last shift. Her family needed her. As she entered, Tess was coming in from the back looking tired around the eyes. Recovering from a late one, no doubt.

"Hi Tess. Have a good night?"

Tess leaned in close. "God, I wish I had a time machine so I could go back to last night and kill myself just before half-eleven."

"That bad?"

Tracy appeared from the kitchen.

"Hello Laura. Last day today. Are you sure you

couldn't do another couple of weeks?"

"Ah no, sorry. How's your mum?"

"She's much better, thanks. I think we'll have to take another member of staff on though. Once the six weeks holiday comes around…"

Tracy gave a little shudder.

Laura sympathized. The school holidays would see Sandy Bay bursting at the seams.

*

A couple of hours later, following a busy lunchtime, Laura emerged from the upstairs bathroom to find Liz on the landing.

"Ah Laura – I couldn't borrow you for a minute, could I?"

"Of course. What is it?"

"I need to get some bedding down from the wardrobe."

She followed Liz to a bedroom. Inside, there was a single bed stripped bare, an empty bookcase, and a wardrobe. An old-fashioned travel trunk sat on top of the wardrobe, out of Liz's reach.

"I normally push the bed across and stand on it," she explained.

"Not with your crocked back, you don't."

Laura used Liz's method and soon had the trunk on the bed. Inside were a duvet, bedsheets and pillows.

"You know my son, Matt, don't you. Tracy said you've spoken to him on the computer."

"Yes, he helped me with something."

"He stays here when he visits. Only I wasn't expecting him."

"Oh, is he coming?"

"Yes, a sudden change of plan – which is strange because he's on holiday in Spain and he's due back at work in Warwick on Monday."

He changed his plans?

Laura's heart rose… and then sank again. If this was solely for her… the woman he assumed to be an islander from East Cowes…

She turned away from Liz. The window offered a view of the outdoor seating area and, to the right, a little of the estuary.

No, he probably just wanted to check on Liz after her bad back episode.

Yes, that was it.

When she turned back, Liz gave her a pillow.

"Could you put a slip on that for me?"

Liz had already put the bottom sheet on and was getting to grips with the duvet.

Laura felt weird. She couldn't say to Matt: 'I've been in your room, touching your pillow.' It would sound like one of those Stephen King novels that Clive the Creep read.

She placed the finished pillow on the bed and gave Liz a hand with the duvet.

"He's a psychiatrist. You must be very proud of him."

"I've always been proud of him. And Tracy. They've worked their socks off."

"It's nice to hear."

Liz dropped her side of the duvet.

"Just wait there…"

Laura looked bemused, but carried on stuffing the duvet into its cover.

Liz returned brandishing a photo album.

"Now, Matt's older by five years," she said as she opened it. "There he is as a baby… and at two… and at five, where Tracy makes her first appearance."

"They're lovely, Liz."

As Liz turned the pages, Laura pretended to be fascinated by all the photos, but her eyes were solely on Matt until…

That's him! The boy!

"That's a nice one," she said, hoping to hold up Liz's progress through the years. It was one of Matt in his scout's uniform.

"He was eleven then. He loved the scouts. They were always out camping, rock climbing, potholing… He also did volunteer work for the elderly."

This guy's a cliché.

Matt was no Clive. He had clearly always been a really nice person. Laura just couldn't stop herself warming to him even more.

"I won't bore you with all of them," said Liz. She went to the last page, where the only photo was of Matt in a green and white soccer kit. It looked quite recent.

"It was a charity game," said Liz. "Last year."

"He looks in good shape," said Laura. "Now, how about we finish the bed?"

They soon had the bed ready and Laura returned the trunk to the top of the wardrobe.

"So which came first?" she asked. "The café or the souvenir shop?"

"Oh, well… right at the start I had a different souvenir shop. I took it over from my parents. I had to buy it from them with a bank loan, mind you. That was their pension. Anyway, it went wrong and I lost the shop."

"Oh. Circumstances can be cruel."

"Yes, especially when 'circumstances' has a name and becomes your fiancé."

"Oh."

"I was young and in love, so I believed all his talk of making it in the big time in London. He worked at Hopton's and thought he could make it as a TV entertainer. He was... well, he was great fun, but a dreamer. I've no idea where he is now."

"It can't have been easy."

"After he left, it took me fifteen years to save up enough money to go again. That's when I started the café. Then, a good few years later, I took over the souvenir shop next door."

"You're a marvel, Liz. You really are. So, you married someone else?"

"Yes, my Joe. We met at the festival watching Jimi Hendrix and were married three months later. He died the same day as David Bowie, so we played Purple Haze and Heroes at his funeral."

Laura loved Liz's story but hated herself for doing stupid calculations that told her Matt was born before Liz met Joe, and that the despicable Hopton's employee was likely to be Matt's dad.

"So... Matt's in Spain with someone called Robbie? He sounds a laugh."

"Don't mention him to Tracy. They were together for seven years but Robbie wouldn't be pinned down."

Ah.

Laura took a last look around Matt's room. Her eyes tried to skim quickly past the bed, but halted there a moment too long.

*

Laura checked the clock. It was nearing four-thirty. Her time at the Moorings was coming to end. In so many ways, she had enjoyed it.

163

Just then, two lovebird customers came in from the back and bade her farewell as they stepped into the street. They had been sitting outside for over an hour, talking low and practically cooing over each other. Laura loved seeing them expressing their affection for each other. She envied them, in a good way.

Maybe me next.

For a moment, she was alone with Tracy.

"So, you and Robbie? A little birdie told me."

"Okay, I'm busted. I do tend to see the worst in Robbie. He's alright though. I just invested too much time in him."

"So he and Matt are good friends?"

"They hardly see each other, but yes. Robbie's on the mainland too – he works in Portsmouth. When they do meet, they spend all day on the golf course."

"So, Planet Robbie…?"

"A slight exaggeration. When they were boys, they owned the shoreline from here to the next bay. From October, right through winter, it was theirs. Then the season would begin and, in the best weather, they wouldn't own it. It would be handed over to strangers who didn't know it like they did."

"I can imagine how that must have felt."

"It made them really solid friends. You'd know. It has to be the same in Cowes."

"Yes."

I am seriously not getting into Heaven.

"Liz told me he plays sport for charity."

"He puts a kit on and runs around, but I don't think he's going to be troubling the Premier League."

Tess was coming in from the back. "I stood in for someone at a charity thing once. They had a celeb come to give prizes and I had to help out with a wine promotion display."

"Who was the celeb?" asked Laura.

"Oh, I can't remember her name. Katie something off the telly. Not a show I ever watched. Anyway, we had this giant inflatable wine bottle. So there's Katie coming in looking all sexy while I'm managing to overinflate the bottle with the electric pump. Next thing, the pressure blows the inflator out of the bottle top and the air thingy rushes out and blows up Katie's summer dress, revealing she doesn't wear knickers."

Laura cracked up. She just wasn't used to having a laugh at work.

"Here," said Tracy. She was proffering an envelope to Laura. "Three days' pay, in cash."

Cash? Better not tell Ross.

"Thanks Tracy. It's been great."

Laura took a ten pound note out of the envelope and popped it in the charity box. That would offset the tax.

"Could I buy you a glass of wine as a personal thank you?" Tracy asked.

"That would be lovely. Thanks."

"Great. Give me ten minutes."

22

Down By The Jetty

#32. Anonymous

Posted 7 years ago

My niece followed in my footsteps as an orange coat. She loves the work and the social life. She's only 22, so doesn't mind (too much) the long hours. I think she's thriving away from home although I hope she can move on in a year or two to less intense work.

It's probably different in many ways from my time in the '90s. For me as a young woman away from home for the first time, it was a bit overwhelming, especially all the drinking and you-know-what that went on. That's just me, of course, and I completely understand why some of the girls I made friends with stayed on for quite a few years!

*

Laura made an excuse to get some fresh air while she waited for Tracy and Tess. The aim was to talk to Matt, if possible.

Standing by the nearest jetty, she watched the boats, the carefree tourists, their stories unfolding. She felt a little like the novelist she was pretending to be.

She Skyped Matt and waited.

A few moments later, his face appeared on her screen.

"I just thought I'd say I've finished at the café and Tracy's taking me out for a glass of wine."

"That's great."

"So…"

"So… there's a bench just up there. We could sit and take in the view."

Weird but nice…

"I was thinking," said Laura. "What about their first fight? In the novel, I mean."

"They fight?"

"They might."

"What would they fight over?"

"I don't know. Maybe he wants a relaxing evening together and she puts on her Best of the Bee Gees CD?"

"What's wrong with that?"

"How would she like it if he put a horror movie on TV? A Stephen King…"

"Why would he put a Stephen King horror movie on TV if they were going to have a romantic evening together?"

"I suppose they don't really know much about each other."

"That's great. I can see that."

"You can?"

"Now they can have fun learning about each other. Maybe they'll be chalk and cheese but feel those two things go so well together."

"Yes, that would be fun."

Having reached the bench, Laura held her phone up

and panned around for Matt to see the view.

"I never tire of it," he said.

She sat down.

"Do you know the castle in Warwick?" he asked.

"I've never actually been."

"We could go there."

Yes! Underground train across London, mainline train from Euston or Paddington or wherever…

"I promise to hold my phone steadier than yours," he said.

"Oh… right…"

He means a bloody video visit.

Her phone rang.

Angela.

"Sorry, Matt, I'll just get rid of my… friend."

"No, it's okay. Call me later."

"How much later."

"As late as you feel safe."

"Oh okay." This would be it. She would tell him how she felt and they could take it from there. "Maybe midnight?"

"Midnight it is."

Laura switched to her boss.

"Hi Angela…"

"Laura, can you think a little more on relationships?"

Good grief – I'm thinking of nothing else!

"Yes, of course, Angela."

23

The Pub

#33: doeadeer

Posted 7 years ago

Hi, I was a waitress at Sandy Bay in 1990 and it was such a good laugh with all the others there. I remember lots of boozy parties in the men's quarters (!!!) and some great nights in the village. I made lots of friends, although this was years before Facebook so I've lost touch. I'm a teacher now – a trusted member of the community. But there was a time when I was so young and free. I simply cannot believe those days are thirty years behind me. It's like Time has made a mistake. Happy, carefree days!

*

In the oven-like late afternoon, Laura arrived at the café doorway to find Tracy finishing the final tidying up of the day.

"I won't be a minute," she called.

Laura moved across to peer into the souvenir shop window, only for the door to open an elderly lady to step out – someone Laura had served a couple of times.

They exchanged a hello before the old timer set off along the street.

Although, a few yards on, before she could be swallowed up among the ambling holidaymakers, she stopped and turned.

"Thank you, Laura," she said.

Laura wasn't quite sure what she was being thanked for. She sensed loneliness though.

"You don't have to thank me. Um… I didn't get your name?"

"It's Georgina. But my friends call me Georgie."

"Well, have a good day, Georgie."

"I know I'm just another holidaymaker," said Georgie, "but I come every year."

"It's a lovely place to come. I hope the weather hasn't been too hot for you."

"The weather does what the weather does. I used to go on holiday with my husband, rain or shine. Not here. He was more a Devon and Cornwall man."

"You get a good cream tea in Devon and Cornwall."

"Yes, he couldn't get enough. I was never quite so bothered. I have tea and cake every day, but cream only once a week. It's so rich, isn't it."

"Yes, I suppose it is."

"Well, listen to me – I'm rambling. I reckon Bill and me had better be going."

Laura's eyes widened a little.

"I'm not mad," said Georgie. "Just a sentimental old fool."

"You're no fool. Not in a million years."

Laura still found it odd to be talking from the position of local worker.

"I bet Bill was a nice man," she said.

"Oh yes, he was. He was always singing. Pop songs, old songs, opera."

Bill reminded Laura of her dad and grandad. They were always singing.

"Not that he had the voice for opera," said Georgie.

"Not many of us do."

"He loved those duets they do. You know. Pavarotti and so on. He bought a couple of CDs. He said you could hear the tears rolling down their cheeks. I liked that. He said he saw a photo once, and they did have tears. Of course, it was acting. I know that. The end of La Boheme, it was. Rodolfo and Mimi. She dies."

"That's often the way in opera."

"Well, I'll be off then. I've taken up more than enough of your time."

"You haven't, honestly."

"You're seaside staff. For us holidaymakers, we get a week or two of you helping to make people's lives better."

"No, really… I'm not actually—"

"Hear me out. You might think your role is a small one, but you're part of a community that helps us to enjoy ourselves, to let our hair down, to recharge our batteries. When we go home we're restored. I should know. I used to work at the seaside hereabouts."

Laura didn't quite follow what she meant, but Liz appeared at the café door.

"Hello Liz," said Laura. "I'm just seeing off a lovely customer of *both* your establishments."

"Hello love," said Liz, addressing a woman of her own age. "What a gorgeous day."

"It certainly is," said Georgie.

"Do come and see us again."

"I will."

They watched the old lady toddle off and merge with her fellow holidaymakers.

"I hear Tracy's taking you out for a glass of wine," said Liz. "Quite right too. You did us a good turn and we're very grateful."

"I'm really glad I did. You look quite well, by the way."

"I'm fine. Back to my best – almost."

"Great." But Laura felt a pang of sympathy. Liz had to be seventy-five.

"Have fun then," said Liz.

"Will do."

Liz disappeared back inside the café to be almost immediately replaced by Tess emerging and squinting against the glare.

"Hello Tess. I wasn't sure if you were still here."

"Cheek. I was tidying up out the back. Tracy won't be long now."

"I was thinking about what you said about office work. I hope you won't be offended, but I could help you put together the best possible CV and find some courses that might help."

"That might be handy."

"It should give you a better chance."

"Okay, thanks. Just email the details to Tracy and I'll get it from her."

"Great."

"Started your diet regime yet?" It was a middle-aged female passer-by in a T-shirt and golf cap.

"Sorry, Pru," said Tess, half-laughing, "I'm too busy to talk to you right now."

Pru laughed right back at her before disappearing into a wine store opposite.

"You're not overweight, are you?" Laura asked. She

thought Tess looked just fine.

"I'm always flirting with a diet," said Tess. "No potatoes one week, no bread the next, and no wine the next. It's nothing serious. Oh, and I was lying about that last one."

Laura smiled. "Very sensible."

"I did try full-on serious dieting once, mind you. The orange and peanut diet."

"You're kidding?" said Laura. "You mean someone came up with a cross between the Mediterranean diet and the squirrel diet?"

"It was a bad time. January, no work, no money, feeling a bit down. You know how it is in the winter. Anyway, I piled on the pounds eating rubbish and drinking too much."

"Even so... that's an extreme diet."

"It did feel a bit weird sitting down to orange juice and peanuts for breakfast. Then it was a jumbo pack of peanuts, two tangerines and a glass of water for elevenses, and then a naval orange, more peanuts, a bottle of orange juice and a pint of water for lunch. I didn't feel sick as such, just mildly poisoned."

"Oh Tess..."

"Same again next day."

"No way."

"It's all true. By then, I was starting to hallucinate. I carried on though. Peanuts and orange juice, yum, yum. By yum-yum, I mean yuck-yuck, because by then it tasted like rabbit droppings washed down with malt vinegar."

"Ugh."

"So, anyway, I'm walking home when my bowels started doing an impression of a washing machine. I thought uh-oh, this could well be a full-scale volcanic eruption with a liquid lava flow. So there's me, running

home, farting along the street, crashing through the front
door, yanking my panties down, thumping my bum onto
the seat and machine-gunning the porcelain."

"That sounds utterly horrific."

"No, I lost five pounds, so I'm happy to recommend
it."

*

It was strange entering the pub, not as a holidaymaker,
but as a worker – if only as a short-term worker who had
just retired from the holiday service industry.

The mood inside was quiet as it was still a little early
and most punters were out the back in the beer garden.
Laura could smell wine and ale and… pie. It was a little
slice of heaven.

At the bar, a cheeky middle-aged man looking cool in
cut-down denim shorts and a Pink Floyd T-shirt smiled at
Tess.

"Still not found Mr Right?" he asked. "Have you
thought about pinning posters on trees?"

"And a good evening to you too, Ted," she replied in
good spirits.

The three workers were soon carrying their glasses of
chilled Pinot Grigio outside, where Laura asked Tess if
she was indeed looking for Mr Right.

"Kind of. To be honest, I'm quite happy assuming the
next guy along is Mr Right. If it turns out he's not, well…
as long as it was fun, eh?"

"That's very profound," said Tracy.

"Keep life simple," said Tess. "That's my take on it.
Next time you see a potential Mr Right, just say hello."

"So that's where I've been going wrong," said Laura.

"Be careful though," warned Tess. "I've just dumped a

right weirdo. Five Shades of Grim."

"No…" said Laura, instinctively moving a little closer.

"Three weeks I'd been seeing him, and so there's me going round to his place and he's wearing a smart suit with a posh silk tie. Oh, are we going out, I said. Call me Mr Grey, he said. He reckoned he'd been to a lot of trouble getting the right suit and everything. Anyway, next thing, I'm tied up on the bed and he's asking how I feel about being covered in melted chocolate. Apparently, there's a video on YouTube. Have you seen it?"

"No," said Laura. Tracy was too busy giggling to answer.

"Anyway, I said, are you insane? And he said, I thought you liked chocolate. Well, yeah, I said – eating it, not wearing it."

Laura cringed.

"Anyway, long-story-short," said Tess, "he says I have the safe word if I want him to stop. Well, I can't remember the bloody safe word. He was always changing it. So he's pouring a tub of warm brown goo over me and I'm shouting California! So he's says that's not the safe word. So I'm shouting, Florida! Texas! Alaska! And he thinks I'm enjoying it. So I'm shouting Oregon! Idaho. And he produces a second tub."

Laura couldn't stop laughing.

"What happened?" she gasped.

"I got there in the end. Ohio. I mean how was I supposed to remember that?"

Laura felt her own life had been far more sheltered than she'd assumed.

"Tess, Tess," said Tracy. "Here's a nice bloke."

She was indicating a man in his forties in a smart pale blue shirt over tan chinos. He was striding their way across the small green.

"Ah," said Tess, having turned to look. "If I'm not mistaken, it's Mr Right."

Laura chuckled. Her former co-worker was unstoppable.

"Hello Baz," said Tess. "How's the boat hire doing?"

"Hello Tess. Very well, thanks. Can I get you a drink?"

"A glass of white wine, please. Just a small one. Unless yours is a big one."

Once again, Laura cringed.

"Two large white wines it is," said Baz, heading for the bar.

"See you later, girls," said Tess, going off to join him.

"I really admire her," said Laura. "The eternal optimist. I really wish her well. Who knows, one day fate might deliver the actual Mr Right. Why not today?"

"Yes, why not," said Tracy.

"She mentioned trying for office work. I said I'd be happy to help her put together a proper CV and look up some courses she could take."

"Tess won't take any courses."

"No?"

"I advised all that two years ago, then one year ago, then three months ago…"

"Ah."

"Last time, I even signed her up to a course and drove her to the first session."

"Oh. How many sessions did she last?"

"One."

"Right."

"Thanks for caring about her though. She's a good friend. I've known her since we were kids."

Laura raised her glass. "Well, best of luck to her. Whatever she does."

"Yeah, good ol' Tess."

"And good ol' us too."
They clinked glasses.
"To the future," said Tracy.
"And whatever it brings," added Laura.

24

The Restaurant and After The Restaurant

#34. Kieran Emery

Posted 7 years ago

Hey everyone! I got through the Hopton's auditions to become an orange coat three years ago. It was like being on the X Factor - nerve-wracking! I sang 'Those Lazy, Hazy, Crazy Days of Summer' and did a silly/happy dance to go with it. They offered me Sandy Bay! Three years on, I absolutely love the place. I take charge of the karaoke and murder all the classics until the holidaymakers have had enough and take over. I also do a bit of DJ-ing. It's such great fun watching families creating special memories all around you. People ask if I ever get tired of smiling, but I honestly love everything about my job.

Freddie Archer replied 7 years ago

What a wonderful post, Kieran. I had your enthusiasm when I was younger, but I suspect not your talent. I never made it to orange coat, so I happily worked in the bar and the kitchen at the Sandy Bay camp. I always admired the orange coats. They were a class apart. There was one during my time, many years ago. She could sing and dance and make people laugh. Such a talent Georgie was. When my wife was alive, she often commented on how selfless the orange coats were and I think she was right.

*

Laura was finding the relaxing meal at the fish restaurant far from relaxing, despite the quiet ambience and the classic warmth of a candle shoved into the top of an old wine bottle. She had earmarked it as a great opportunity to start work on being buddies with Ross. Only, her impending late night video call to Alicante was jostling for position with her fears of becoming Arnold. Maybe Ross was the kind of the man who preferred distance. Maybe it wasn't something that could ever be overcome.

On her third glass of wine, she supposed it had to be worth some effort. If she was to have a meaningful relationship with Amy and Evie, it would be better if she and Ross could find some common ground.

Her series of questions about his office seemed to go off the rails somehow. Asking about who he worked with focused on a woman called Jenna, which crashed heavily when Laura wondered if he saw more of her than Amy and Evie.

Undeterred, Laura turned to the ultra-sports that Ross enjoyed but unintentionally brought up all the women doing triathlon alongside him.

More wine followed, mainly to calm her rising worry about what would happen during her video call. Exactly what did people do?

And more questions went across the table at Ross.

Finally, he snapped.

"Laura, this feels a bit like an interrogation."

"I'm just trying to be friends," she said, pouring herself more wine. "Friends should make the extra effort. If you have a problem, you can share it with friends."

"I don't have a problem."

"Now, come on, Ross. It's nothing to be ashamed of."

"What??"

"Try to avoid excess alcohol. That never helps."

Ross looked furious. "I *do not* have a problem. Okay?"

"He doesn't," Amy confirmed.

"Oh, then I've got hold of the wrong end of the stick."

"This is no time for innuendo," said Harry.

"I'm so sorry," said Laura, leaning across the table to pat him, thereby knocking over the candle, which splashed molten white wax onto his groin making it look like the aftermath of a sex accident.

That, apparently, was the final straw.

*

In bed, alone. Laura's nightie was beginning to cling to her skin. The window was open, which let in a little of the cool night air, but also the voices of those returning from a later night out than she'd had.

She stared at the phone in her sweaty hand. It felt more like a barrier than a portal. She wanted to see him... to feel her skin against his skin, not against an unyielding plastic screen.

She checked the time.

11:55 p.m.

She made the call.

He wouldn't be busy discussing golf with Robbie, would he?

Matt appeared on the screen. He was in his room.

"I wasn't sure if you'd call," he said.

"Are you happy I did?"

"I'm always happy to see you, Laura."

"I thought you might be talking about golf with Robbie."

"Not right now, no."

"I don't get golf. You hit a little ball into a little hole."

"Okay, so half my games I play alone. I spend three hours on the course. About ten minutes of that is hitting a little ball into a little hole. The rest is me and my thoughts roaming free in the open countryside. If I need company, I play with a friend and we get to talk. Not drunk talk like in a bar, but considered talk with occasional pauses to reflect on what we've said while we hit a little ball into a little hole. Don't you think hitting a little ball into a little hole is a small price to pay for all that quality time?"

"Golf sounds okay."

She wanted to brush her fingers across his cheek, but knew that would seem weird as all he'd see was a big hand blocking his view.

This was so strange. Free from anything she might later regret happening, she wanted everything to happen. It was a feeling she didn't quite know what to do with.

She could feel his lips on hers – even though she couldn't.

She could feel his breath on her neck – even though that was impossible.

This was hotter than any lovemaking she'd ever experienced. It was so intense. Too intense.

She felt foolish and exhilarated. She also knew, one hundred percent, if he walked into the room right now, she would drag him into the bed and go wild.

And that wasn't her at all.

What was happening to her? She was fifty-two. At that age, she had earned the right to have some control over her hormones.

Hormones?

She wondered – did she even have any left?

This was the moment. She would tell him how she felt. "Matt…"

"I'm coming back to the island," he said.

Yes, I know. "Really? When?"

"My flight gets into Gatwick at half-eleven Saturday morning."

Great. "Then you'll head straight to the ferry."

"No, then I'll go home to Warwick to sort a few things out. I should be on the ferry Monday lunchtime."

"Oh, we'll be on the boat home by then."

"Boat home? I thought you lived locally."

"Yes… no."

"Yes, no?"

"I lied."

"You lied?"

"I'm not from the Isle of Wight."

"What? But…"

"I'm a liar, Matt. Oh crap, what am I saying? This is Ross's fault for getting me drunk."

"Ross?"

"Oh f… goodbye, Matt. Goodbye. Sorry. The novel was a lie too!"

The Skype session was over.

Her face hit the pillow.

Then she prayed for a deep sleep that wasn't likely to happen anytime soon.

25

Crazy Golf

#35: janetcollinswasmajor

Posted 7 years ago

I worked at Sandy Bay in the 60s. The head orange coat was a man called Ralph – it's probably the same Ralph someone else mentioned. He'd been in the army during the War, serving in the Far East. He was very young and saw a lot of bad things, which I think made him double-determined that everyone visiting Sandy Bay would have a great time, including himself. He worked all the hours and nothing was too much trouble. Those were very happy, carefree days.

*

Laura dragged her sorry carcass out of bed to make a much-needed mug of coffee.

"Three hours' sleep," she muttered. It was June. The days were long. And they damn well felt it.

She checked her phone. It was off. Well, it could stay off.

While the kettle boiled she freshened up in the

bathroom and tried not to be too hard on herself.

"Hello Arnold," she said to the mirror. "Holiday romances aren't meant to last and families are always arguing, okay?"

A few moments later, sitting in the lounge with the patio doors wide open, she sipped her coffee and continued with her efforts to rationalize the whole thing away.

Okay, okay…

Did she want to become Arnold?

Stupid question.

Did she want to bring her family together as friends?

Yes.

Could she achieve that in the remaining window of Friday, Saturday and Sunday?

Er…

Or would they achieve a last-minute collective nirvana during Monday's journey home?

Next question.

So, Matt… did a meaningful adult relationship need to be with that particular individual?

Definitely not.

Had their chance meeting, and all the video calls, merely forced open a long-closed door?

Yes, the total humiliation was worth it.

Was the new mission to fix her life after this holiday, when she'd be working 24/7 for Angela?

Unfair question.

Laura stepped out onto the patio and breathed in the morning air with its hint of grass and sea. The sun was up and the temperature would soon follow. It was going to be another scorching day.

"Here I am, world," she said. "Laura Cass reporting for duty."

*

An hour later, the whole family was having breakfast. A waffle here, oat flakes there, a bacon sandwich somewhere else. Laura was on the patio, another coffee in hand, staring out to the distant horizon on the sea.

She wondered what the next step should be. Perhaps an activity they could all do, where they would also get a chance to talk.

She thought of Matt.

Specifically, Matt hitting a little ball into a little hole – that gave people a chance to play, to ponder alone, and to converse at length.

Golf really did seem a much better game than she'd previously imagined. The only problem would be dragging her non-golfing family around a massive course in a heatwave. Perhaps the family holiday version would do instead?

"Does anyone fancy a game of crazy golf?" she asked.

She waited for a flood of negativity.

"Crazy golf?" said Ross, mulling it over. "Good call."

"I'm ready to beat all-comers," said Harry.

Amy and Bev were also nodding.

"Crazy golf it is then," said Laura. "Now we just need to find a course."

She would have thanked Matt for giving her the idea, but he was history and love was just a bunch of chemicals.

"Here's one," said Ross, studying his phone. "It looks like it's on some old pier."

"This just gets better and better," said Harry. "There's nothing like a sea breeze to make shots harder."

"Brilliant," said Laura. She switched her phone on.

Maybe Matt had texted.

Angela had texted. And emailed. Something about a Head Teacher in London.

A Google calendar alert popped up.

"Oh crap – my call!"

Her family watched in bemusement as Laura threw on a smart top and dragged a brush through her hair while she fired up her laptop for a video call booked to begin five minutes ago.

*

Standing on the pier, Laura stared out to sea. The slight breeze was unlikely to disturb the quality of the golf, but it would keep them cool under pressure.

She was relieved to have put a half hour video call behind her, along with a one hour rewriting session to tailor the content more to the school's requirements. Now, after a ten minute drive from Sandy Bay, she finally felt the freedom that most holidaymakers wake up with.

"It looks a tough course," said Harry.

Laura joined him in studying the windmill hole, the Disney castle hole and the long pipe hole.

"It certainly does," she concurred.

At the shack where they would pay and collect their putters and balls, Bev and Amy unexpectedly decided to sit out this great sporting event.

"Mum, you can handle the boys," said Amy.

Hmm, a conspiracy?

The game started well – with plenty of terrible shots and much laughter. Especially when Laura's shot jumped the twelve-inch perimeter and flew out of the exit towards the burger hut.

Then Ross admitted that the restaurant candle wax

disaster had been funny.

"Thank God no one filmed it," he said. "YouTube would have gone wild."

Next, Laura tried to channel Matt playing golf. Would he miss the dinosaur's mouth from two feet?

"Oh, bad luck," said Ross.

The game was soon over, but Laura was keen to go again.

"Come on, Amy. You and me."

Bev obliged by taking Evie for a stroll in the buggy with the parasol raised and plenty of juice at the ready. Harry and Ross went to lean against the rail looking out over the beach and shoreline of breaking waves.

Amy rose to face her challenger.

"Mum, I've not seen you like this since… since forever. You're like Mum of old."

Laura took a moment to take in her daughter's observation. Mum of old and Amy had been inseparable friends.

"I do feel a little more relaxed," she said. "Maybe family holidays aren't such a bad idea. This one's started to make me realize what I've been missing out on."

"I wouldn't want us to drift apart, Mum."

"That will never happen, Amy."

"I don't mean physically. I mean… our bond. Our friendship."

"I know what you mean."

Amy brightened. "Do you remember when we used to go ten-pin bowling?"

"Yes, I do."

"I used to love that."

"Yes… and now we're back as deadly rivals, but this time it's with smaller balls."

They played and had fun – and Laura appreciated the

real point of playing crazy golf with loved ones.

"Mum, you're a sensible person," Amy said, halfway round the course.

"I'm a what?"

"A sensible person."

"Amy, I no longer hold that office. They took my badge away, tore up my certificate, and threw me out of the institute."

"Thing is," said Amy, "I'm not sure where we're going to live."

Ah...

Amy took her shot. Her ball stopped short of the hole.

Laura felt the heat rising. Although it was only eleven a.m., the temperature later was due to be around 34 degrees Celsius – well over 90 Fahrenheit. She took her shot.

"Wow, a hole in one," she gasped. "I'll be available for autographs later."

Amy took her next shot – and missed the dinosaur's mouth from two feet.

"So we're thinking of moving to the coast."

"Oh..." Laura chose not to mention Harry's tip-off. "I think that's a great idea."

"You do?"

"It'll be great for Evie, and it'll be great for you and Ross. Whoever's idea it was, you have my one hundred percent support."

"Thanks Mum."

"And I hope we can be friends. I'd like to keep in touch. And I don't mean via a screen."

"We *are* friends."

"No, I mean real friends. Mum of old and Amy friends who do stuff together, who have a laugh together, who share their sorrows. You know – the opposite of how I've treated you and Ross over the past few years."

"You've been busy at work. Angela can't build a business from scratch without massive support. You've been a rock."

"I'd just like us to be two twits playing ten-pin bowling again, Amy. That's all."

"Perhaps when you retire?"

"That's a decade and a half away."

Laura's phone rang. She checked the screen.

"Sorry, Amy… you go on ahead."

Laura answered the call.

"Angela, hi…"

"Laura, I'm calling from a public phone. We have an emergency situation."

"God, what – is the office on fire?"

"No, someone stole my iPhone."

"Oh… that's bad. Are you okay?"

"I'm fine. It was a moped thief. They just rode by and grabbed it from my hand."

"That must have been a shock."

"It was."

"Well, as long as you're not hurt. That's the main thing. What will you do – just get another one, I expect."

"Yes, but that'll take time and I need you to look at a contract on the system – and pronto, please."

"Wouldn't it be easier for you to do it from the office computer?"

"Laura, I'm in Paris and I haven't got my iPhone."

"Paris? The *French* Paris?"

"Yes, Laura, I'm having a few days away. Could you take over for a bit? I need a contract looked at quite soon. Very soon. Now-ish. If you could…?"

"But I'm away for a few days too. Ten of them, in fact."

"Laura, I'm currently a tourist without phone, so there's no point in arguing. Write down this password and go into the secure part of the system. Have you got a pen?"

Laura took a pen and pad from her bag and jotted down the details. It annoyed her that Angela couldn't simply buy another phone and load up all the bits and pieces necessary to run the business from it. The client would understand the delay.

Five minutes later, having accessed the website through her phone and emailed the client, Laura looked to resume the game – only Amy had finished and had joined Ross and Harry at the railing overlooking the beach.

"What's the plan?" she called.

They turned and Harry smiled.

"Me and you," he said.

A moment later, they were going round the course again.

"You're keen," said Laura.

"It's a chance to talk one to one," said Harry.

"Oh?"

"Take your shot."

Laura did so and missed. Three shots later, she completed the hole.

"So what's on your mind, Harry?"

"It's more to do with what's on *your* mind."

"How do you mean?"

They started the next hole.

"Romance is a big part of life," said Harry. "Don't deny yourself just because The Man From La Mancha didn't work out."

"How do you know that?"

"You stare out to sea a lot."

"Yes, well, I'm done with the whole relationship thing. I don't need it."

"You will though. In time. It's the elephant in the room. Or at least the elephant that left the room. They're the worst. You can't ignore those. Especially when they come back into the room."

"Harry, I'm going to set you free. Like they do with knackered old donkeys. You'll enjoy having a field all to yourself. "

Harry laughed. "I'd only let a friend talk to me like that."

Laura stopped. "Are we friends?"

"Yes, we are," said Harry. "Now… in which desolate part of Britain is this field?"

*

An hour or so later, having raided a deli for supplies to bring back for lunch, the family members were making their way from the car back to the chalet.

"I'm starving," said Harry. "All that victorious golf has sharpened my appetite."

"I can't think why they don't put crazy golf on TV," said Amy.

"I'm ready to sign a multi-million dollar deal if they do," said Harry. "You lot could be my fans. The Harryettes."

As they neared their holiday home, Laura's gaze was drawn away from Chalet 44. Outside Chalet 45, the teen girl was waving off her parents. And even before they were out of sight, she was making a call.

Then a family new to Laura came walking by. Two young people with young children, all hand in hand. They exchanged hellos and Laura could only admire them.

Young love. A young family. At such a wonderful time in their lives. She hoped they realized it. Because it was easy to let the years slip by and end up feeling you got it wrong somehow.

26

The Write Stuff

#36: paddycoyneinkent

Posted 6 years ago

Hi, is anyone still following this thread? It's a year since any comments. Anyway, I went to Sandy Bay many times as a kid. I remember Ralph the chief orange coat. He was the best and actually inspired me to get into the business – I was a red coat at Butlin's for ten years. I'm Facebook friends with a retired orange coat who knew Ralph. Unfortunately, he passed away in 2001 (self-inflicted, unfortunately). It feels like a heavy weight to know that a life & soul guy like Ralph is long gone and largely forgotten.

*

While lunch was being laid out on the dining table, Laura was in her room, going over a couple of unclear sentences in the contract. It had taken will power to ignore another document on her laptop – the notes for her fake novel. That was something she missed – discussing her non-novel with Matt. It had been good to get a collaborative view of the male-female dynamic.

She wondered. What if she were to continue with it? Not the fake non-novel, but a real one?

She opened the notes and considered an important question.

Did the Main Female Character's story have a satisfying romantic challenge? According to the notes, she liked two men: Male #1 and Male #2.

Tough choice.

"Lunch, Laura," Bev called from the main room.

"Won't be a mo."

Could she write a novel, for real, in the three spare minutes she had each week? At that rate it would take her the rest of the century to finish it. Although, once she'd retired…

So, that's when she'd have time for her family and herself.

What about all the precious years in between?

What about *now*?

Maybe she could talk to Matt. Maybe she could say it was one final, final chat – simply to clear the air. She could say she didn't want him thinking the worst of her. Stress and burnout had got to her. What sort of psychiatrist would he be if he didn't understand that?

Laura noticed she hadn't shut down the secure part of the system. That might have been forgetfulness, or possibly curiosity. But any thought of peeking at other secret files was cut short by activity outside her window. Chalet 45 activity, no less. She moved closer to the window and watched the teen girl let a teen boy inside.

Laura shut down the laptop and left the room.

"Take a plate, Laura," said Bev.

"I won't be a minute, Mum."

She went out onto the communal green.

MARK DAYDY

The grass was hot and dry under her bare feet.

Ahead lay Chalet 45.

This is bad.

The sun above was unforgiving. Its dazzle was even worse bouncing back at her off the white chalet wall. She felt like Clint Eastwood in a spaghetti western. Should she call out a warning, perhaps?

Put those naughty bits away and come out with your hands up.

Approaching the front door took her back thirty-five years. There was a boy. Nick. He had that amazing smile. And although he was only eighteen, he was so confident.

She blocked the memory.

Not while I'm on duty as a responsible adult.

The door flew open and out popped the girl and the boy carrying a picnic cooler box.

"Oh?" said the girl.

"Oh?" said Laura, standing far too close. "I thought I… saw something."

"Oh," said the girl again. "We're off to the beach."

"Great," said Laura, stepping back to let them by.

Young love.

Such a wonderful time.

She too had the strongest urge to share a picnic.

*

Laura was working her way through an oversized, overstuffed Cheddar cheese salad sandwich with zero enthusiasm.

"Not hungry, love?" Bev asked.

"No, I'm… yum…"

She took another bite.

She'd be back in the office on Tuesday. Something important was going to slip away. As she chewed, she

196

fantasized about a boy and a girl having a picnic on the beach. It was all very innocent. But then the boy and girl morphed into Matt and Laura and they were alone on a deserted shoreline. And she was in his arms. And in tune with him. And in rhythm with him. And she could feel the tension building…

"Are you alright, Laura?" said Harry. "You look like you're in pain."

Laura sipped some water and started to make plans for next year. A weekend away with Bev and Harry. Visits to Amy, Ross and Evie. She'd book a hotel if they didn't have space for her at their home on the coast. She'd talk to Angela too. Yes, the business required long hours and a serious commitment, but Saturdays and Sundays, and holiday breaks simply had to be ring-fenced. And yet, she knew that wouldn't happen. There was a lot of work in the pipeline.

She sighed. It had been a strange break. Ten days of total rest and relaxation?

Not quite.

Still, if holidays were about making memories, she had certainly made a few of those. Nearly getting into serious trouble with Clive the Creep. That was one memory she hoped would fade. And then there was Matt, the fantasy boy who became a psychiatrist and flew to Spain.

She made an excuse and withdrew to her room. Romance was a fool's game, but business was a different matter. She couldn't write a novel, but she could get some work done on how to deliver relationship guidance for teens.

She paused… and pondered her first holiday love.

Nick…

Her thoughts drifted back thirty-five years to a chalet bedroom at a holiday camp on the mainland… in

Cornwall… a fishing village… his body poised above hers. And Bev unexpectedly returning and calling "do you want tea?" And Nick plunging in all the same. And that first-time gasp at the feel of him. And that sense of amazed fulfilment… for ten seconds before he grunted, rolled off, got dressed, and disappeared via the window. She never saw him again.

He'd been in his mid-fifties now.

For no particular reason, she accessed the secure part of the company website and took a good look around.

"Interesting," she mused.

27

King of the Castle

#37: moose

Posted 6 years ago

Hi raceboyrogers (Ed?). I remember you and Ralph doing Singing in the Rain. I worked as an all-round entertainer at Sandy Bay in 1979 and 80. I really thought I might make a career of it and it was all I could think of (apart from the lovely Carrie, of course!). I have so many wonderful, crazy memories. Ralph as Elvis was unforgettable. I'm a retired lawyer these days, living in Florida with my American wife. We have two sons in their 30s who have never been to England.

Anon replied 6 years ago

Ralph was great fun but you should also remember he had problems with drink and gambling going back to the early 1960s. I heard he wasted his fiancée's money and ruined her business, and then left her. The poor girl was twenty years younger than him (impressionable?) and had to work hard for years to save the money to start another business. I heard even her son had to work in a café when he was eleven.

*

After lunch, the family headed off to the Roman villa at Newport. They were surprised to find it tucked between so many modern houses. It seemed out of place, even though it had been there 1,700 longer than any of the newer homes.

While they were studying the Roman bath, Harry gave Laura a knowing glance and then moved in on Ross. He mentioned how it was a big thing for Roman fathers to guide their children. It seemed they did so from a very young age.

A little later, Laura got to Harry in private.

"Is that true?" she asked.

"No idea," said Harry.

They finished their tour and made their way to their next stop, Carisbrooke Castle, located just over a mile away. Having parked the car, they strolled through the 900-year-old gatehouse into the castle grounds.

"What a lovely place," said Bev.

"Yes," said Harry, "it's where Charles the First was held before they took him away to be executed."

"I'm sure there are happier memories here," said Amy.

Laura took in the crumbling walls and old staircases. According the website, the views from the higher points went as far as the Solent.

A middle-aged female guide smiled at her. Laura smiled back.

A local worker. Engage with her.

"Do you live locally?" she asked.

"I do now," said the guide. "I'm originally from Swindon. When I was a kid, we used to come here on family holidays. I loved it so much I once hid so we'd miss the ferry home. They found me in a cupboard just in time."

"So making the move was a no-brainer."

"Yes, I loved seeing our kids grow up here. They did more than most children could dream of and the people are so friendly."

"I think you're a testament to that," said Laura.

She went off to find the rest of her family – and almost stumbled across Bev and Harry seated in a quiet spot. Bev was taking a mint from his pack and laughing at something he'd said. It made Laura smile. Her mum hadn't married a bad man.

She opted for a noisy entrance rather than admit to being a spy.

"Is that a mint I see before me?"

Harry obliged.

"We just needed a break," Bev explained. "It's getting hard to keep up."

"You stay there a bit longer then," said Laura. "I'll check on the others."

Sucking on a mint, she headed off, refusing to countenance her mum coming to the end of the road – or conveyor belt. Instead, she reflected on where she was with Ross and Amy.

She soon found them – high up but apart, looking out over the surrounding countryside. Laura joined Amy in a shady spot and made a fuss of baby Evie, who was looking cool under her pushchair's parasol. Ross was farther on, surveying his kingdom, perhaps.

"You'll never guess what Ross has been looking at on his phone," said Amy. "I saw it when he was in the shower."

Laura felt dread. "I hope you're going to say it's a cute kittens website."

"No, it's relationship problems. I asked him about it but he dismissed it as nothing. What do you think?"

"What do I think?"

"Gran said I should ask you."

"Did she?"

"Mum, the holiday's nearly over. We're going home soon. I hardly sleep. I hardly bloody talk about anything that isn't baby-related. I'm very attracted to Ross, but it's just not working right now."

Laura left London hoping this would be a happy family holiday. Now Ross and Amy were fighting while Harry and Bev teetered on the edge of the conveyor belt of life like a couple of geriatric James Bonds. Throw in a holiday romance with a man in the wrong country...

"You're not the only one, Amy. Millions of men go through this. It passes though. I know he denied it in the restaurant, but if you work together as a team, he'll... um, rise to the occasion."

"What?"

"I'm not going to spell it out graphically."

"What are you talking about? Ross was telling the truth. He doesn't have a problem. It's me."

"You? But it's Ross who always looks so frustrated."

"Yes, because since the birth, I've not been able to... get where a woman needs to get."

"Oh."

"He refuses to have his moment when I'm not able to have mine. He says it has to be me first and foremost getting there otherwise it's not fair. So what do you think?"

"Well, I think you should definitely hang on to him!"

Laura thought back to Jonathan. Had he even noticed that she didn't ever…

"Mum, he's got this bedtime notion that if he can't make me happy, he's failed. It's making us both unhappy."

"Yes, well, that's… yes…"

Laura reminded herself that she helped teachers find ways to deliver sensitive relationship guidance without embarrassment or awkwardness – it was just that she couldn't recall any of it right now.

Amy stared out across the castle grounds.

"People said I was lucky not to have post-natal depression, but I've had post-natal total exhaustion and loss of sex drive, plus Ross not getting involved with Evie and constantly arranging things that aren't baby related, like stupid paintball wars. My libido has crashed, I'm breastfeeding, my body isn't ready for action, it's all a total mess."

"Have you seen a doctor?"

"She said it'll pass. Just keep talking. She didn't want to put me on drugs, but I just feel so stressed and tired."

"Have you googled it?"

"A million times. Take a hot shower and get some meaningful sleep. And do non-sex things like watch TV together in an embrace."

"And you're doing that?"

"The hot shower, yes."

For a brief moment, Laura thought of contacting Matt for his professional opinion, but her own difficulties with Jonathan came creeping back. She read a lot of books about it back then. None of it impressed Jonathan, but the advice was probably still sound. With the holiday almost over, and the prospect of Amy and Ross drifting apart, she wracked her brains.

"Okay, here are some thoughts. It could be you're not responding to Ross because he's not tightly bonded to *your* baby – the baby who means the world to *you*. It could be that Ross is struggling with the reality of being a dad. It could be that he's waiting for his turn to start bonding with Evie."

"His turn? She's nearly five months old."

"Yes, look, I'm not an expert, but I went through something similar with your father. Believe me, I read my way through a library on the subject. The thing is, some new dads can feel like interlopers... you know, like they're breaking in on the perfect bond between mother and baby. That's why they hold off getting fully involved."

"So Dad had the same problem as Ross?"

No, lovely Dad had no trouble banging away regardless.

"No, your dad and me... we... weren't like you and Ross. Um, do you feel you're leaving him enough space to get fully involved with Evie?"

"Mum, he can have all day with her. I would be so happy with that."

"But he doesn't."

"No."

"Do you want me to talk to him?"

"I don't know. Probably. Yes. If you wouldn't mind. You seem to be friends."

"Do we?"

"Well, you protect him from Harry."

"Oh... right."

She looked to Ross, a little way along the castle wall, looking very Highlander.

"Okay, I'm going in."

She strode off, attempting to look calm yet purposeful, friendly yet mentor-like.

"How's it going?" she puffed as she caught up with him. "I was reading an article recently. About new dads."

"Oh?"

"Amazing insight into some of the very common problems that men hide away."

"Okay…?"

"Quite a lot of men find the reality of parenting doesn't line up with the expectations they had."

"Thanks, but I'll handle it."

"Yes, so, even though it's none of my business, there's just enough time left before the holiday ends for us to become friends."

"Is this Harry's idea?"

"I honestly can't remember. The thing is, this family has been broken for decades, but we're fixing it now. You don't need me telling you how to live your life, but you need to get fatherhood right."

"If you must butt in…"

"I care about Amy and Evie."

"I said if you *must* butt in…" He seemed to be weighing things up. It took a moment for his next words to form. "You're not wrong."

"Right. Er… how?"

"I just can't seem to find the way in. I buy toys, I make cooing noises, I change her once a day. I just don't feel a bond anything like Amy does."

"Okay…"

"I feel terrible. Basically, I don't know how to be a father. Seriously, I've read tons of stuff on the internet, but I just don't feel right. Between you and me, I think that gets to Amy, because, well… it gets to her and it's not helping us, because… well, she… oh, this is coming out all wrong. I do care, Laura. Please don't think I'm only thinking about me."

"I think you're a very nice young man and I'm glad my daughter found someone who cares like you do."

"Really? Oh, I didn't…"

"Are you the Alphabet Animal Man?"

"Pardon?"

Laura's recollection of a conversation she had with Jonathan twenty-seven years ago had come back to her.

"Are you the Numbers Dance Man?"

"The what?"

"A new dad doesn't have to be amazingly brilliant. He just needs to ditch the Mr Cool T-shirt and some of his ego… and just be a great big silly sausage."

"She's only tiny, Laura. I did think I might slowly introduce a few google ideas as she gets older."

"Ross! Wake up! That's too late. You have to start now."

"But…"

"Focus on your relationships with the *two* most important people in your life, okay? Amy is leaving you all the room you need to be a good dad."

"I just feel like a fake."

"Well, you're not. You're the real thing. A father and his child can be a slower bond to build, but it ends up just as solid. So get building, Ross – just remember what noises animals make and try to put a bit of oomph into your daughter and dad dance routines. And count from one to ten while you're doing it."

Ross seemed to gather himself in.

"I'll try."

Laura looked down into the castle's courtyard. Bev and Harry were talking to the guide.

Yes, the local worker. The helper.

Hopton's suddenly came to mind and Laura had it.

"Did you say you'll try?"

"Yes, I promise."

"Well, that's not good enough, Ross. Okay, listen, from today, you'll be an orange coat."

"Sorry…?"

"I'm not suggesting you get a new job. I mean that's your new role with Evie. You're now her personal, all-year-round orange coat. Just do what they do."

"An orange coat…?"

"Yes, Ross. You'll be using energy and enthusiasm. And a smile."

"That is the silliest…"

"The people who created holiday camps built empires on it."

Laura left Ross and walked by Amy and Evie, with a smile, and went down to join Bev and Harry.

"All alright?" Bev asked.

"I'm just trying to get Ross to be an engaged dad."

"And now he hates you?" wondered Harry.

"We'll soon find out."

A moment later, Ross emerged, holding Evie, and dancing like a loon. He seemed to be making animal noises.

"Oh no," said Harry. "He's had a total breakdown."

"No," said Laura, "he's being an orange coat."

"He thinks that?" said Harry. "It's worse than I thought."

Amy emerged, looking happy. She smiled at Laura.

"Ross is singing Old MacDonald," said Bev. "Oh, how lovely. Let's all join in."

"Not me," said Harry.

"Yes, you too," said Bev.

Laura was happy to sing along with a moo-moo here and a baa-baa there, and laugh at Ross's antics. If that boy could feel an equal parent…

"Well, Ross, you're certainly making Evie laugh," said Bev.

"And Amy too," said Harry.

Perfect, thought Laura. A man who can make his partner laugh was definitely on the right track.

A few minutes later, there was a breathless glow about Ross. Amy kissed Laura's cheek and whispered, "Thanks, Mum."

Laura felt elated.

"I know I'm an old grumbler," Harry told Ross, "but we must never stop doing the right thing for children. Whether they're five years or five months. You're so lucky to be a father. Miracles are waiting for you every single day. Everything's coming your way, Ross. Don't miss a second of it."

Laura couldn't have agreed more. Now it was time to take the next step.

28

Biding Time

#38: alanwilliamson

Posted 5 years ago

I lost my dad back in 1965 when I was 14. Up until then, we used to have a week's holiday each summer. The best place was the holiday camp at Sandy Bay on the Isle of Wight because we had to go on a ferry and I could pretend to be the captain on the lookout for a seaborne Bond villain.

It wasn't until I was 30 that I took my own family to the Isle of Wight – not Sandy Bay, but Shanklin. And guess what, I still imagined being the captain on the lookout for seaborne dangers. Ridiculous, I know. Still, it made my boys laugh (they were 5 and 3 that first time). We took my mum too and it was a bit emotional when we visited the old Sandy Bay camp we previously stayed at. We recalled Dad playing in the campers' football match and scoring a goal. It was a feeble shot that just about rolled over the goal line, but by the time we got home, Dad had struck the ball like a thunderbolt, smashing it thirty yards into the top corner, with all the players agreeing it was the best goal they had ever seen and it was a shame a professional talent scout wasn't there that day.

I thought it would be Mum who cried when we went to look at the chalet we last stayed in, but blow me down, it was me who started. All the years of missing my dad came rushing back and completely overwhelmed me. The strange thing was I thanked the old place. What precious memories.

Freddie Archer replied 5 years ago

Hello everyone. Freddie here. Thank you very much for sharing your story, Alan. Most heartening.

*

They arrived back at Hopton's at three and were walking from the car to the chalet. The five-year-old boy was outside Chalet 43.

Ross immediately ran to retrieve a wayward ball... and brought it back trying to do keepy-uppies in his sandals. The boy laughed.

"What's your name?" Ross asked, awkwardly but genuinely.

"Ashley."

"Come on, Ashley. I'm Ross the goalie, you're the striker. See if you can score a goal."

Ross took up a position in front of Chalet 43's front door. Ashley was brimful of glee, although lacked the skill to score a goal. His shot went wide, but Ross picked it up and...

"Oh no, it was a magic shot... the ball changes

direction… and goal!" yelled Ross having engineered an unlikely success for Ashley.

The door opened to reveal Ashley's dad.

"Oh… Ashley, come and get your beach stuff."

Ross high-fived Ashley and withdrew.

"Thanks Ross!" the boy declared.

Laura could see it in Ross's face. He really did get it. He really did finally understand that all of this was coming his way. And she really did believe he wasn't going to miss a second of it.

Laura made a decision.

She addressed Amy.

"Me, Mum and Harry fancy a walk."

"Do we?" gasped Harry.

Laura cut across him, keeping her focus on Amy. "Why don't we keep Evie with us? You and Ross could… put your feet up for a bit."

"A bit of what?" grumbled Harry.

But Bev hauled Harry back while Laura took control of the baby's buggy.

"We'll be back in two hours," she said.

"Two hours?" Harry gasped once more.

"Shut up and walk," said Bev. "If this is going to be our last family holiday, let's make it a good one."

Laura smiled, but the reality of Bev's words hit home and her smile faded.

*

Laura, Bev, Harry and Evie took a bench by the seafront. The weather was glorious and, for Laura, watching children playing in the gently breaking waves, the world seemed at peace.

"I wasn't trying to stop them," said Harry.

"I know," said Laura.

"I was just exhausted."

"I know."

"Two hours though. I won't be the only one who's exhausted."

"So, Harry, your treatment…?"

"It's nothing," he said.

Bev leaned down under Evie's parasol and pointed out to sea.

"Look at the boat, Evie. Can you see the boat?"

She was referring to a large cruiser a long way from the shore. Laura could see that Evie enjoyed the question, even if an answer was beyond her.

"It's prostate trouble," said Harry. "My equipment's acting up, but it's not the end of the world."

"I see. And what about you, Mum? Anything you're not telling me?"

"There's nothing wrong with me," said Bev. "Apart from my back and leg."

Laura knew all about her mother's condition – for years though to be recurring sciatica but more recently diagnosed as a lumber issue to do with the lower spine. Fortunately, walking was good for it.

"I don't think we'll be able to come again next year," Bev added.

Laura wasn't one for dwelling on everyone getting older, but she knew Bev had bad days and that she was getting more not less of them.

"I've been thinking about next year," she said. "I could always drag you two to Eastbourne for a long weekend. We could book a hotel."

"That's very kind," said Bev. "We'll see."

Laura quite fancied Eastbourne. It wouldn't be far off the family's centenary of first visiting there.

"Anyone fancy an ice cream?" she asked.

Harry and Bev declined, so Laura went off to the shack fifty yards away.

A few minutes later, ice cream in hand, she perched on a bench by the shack to indulge herself and ponder the nature of life and what she might have for dinner. Life, she decided, was a gift, and dinner would be fish at a restaurant overlooking the water.

"Hello. Your day off, is it?"

It was Georgie, the nice old lady she had served in the café.

"Hello."

"I see you've found my bench," said Georgie, sitting down next to her. "This was our place, you know."

"Oh, that's nice."

Laura felt sorry for her, recalling that she'd said her husband Bill never came to Sandy Bay.

"His name was Freddie," Georgie continued. "I think he was too shy to ask me out."

"Ah, this was before Bill..."

"Yes, Freddie wanted to be a children's entertainer. I wanted to be a night club singer. I felt our worlds would be different, so I made myself turn elsewhere. Oh, I was so stupid."

"We're all capable of making mistakes when we're young."

"I'm still making them now. Do you know there was a very nice man at a charity event a couple of years ago and I never spoke to him all evening. Daft, eh? Well, either that or I'm getting too old."

"Nobody's too old for companionship."

"Oh, you think he could have been Mr Right?"

They both laughed. Then something came back to Laura.

"A good friend of mine says we should keep life simple. Next time you see a potential Mr Right, just say hello."

"That's very good advice, Laura."

"Yes, I might use it myself sometime. Well, have a good day, Georgie."

Once Laura rejoined her family, they stayed another twenty minutes, watching the familiar activity of the beach in summer – and with Laura changing a damp Evie.

"Right," said Bev. "Let's look for some knick-knacks. There must be a few more things I can take home as souvenirs."

"You'd better hire a second car to fit them all in," said Harry.

The hunt for knick-knacks was followed by a hunt for cakes. It was another hour before they finally made their way back to the camp.

Approaching their chalet, Harry started coughing theatrically.

Ross came out first, then Amy came out beside him, practically glowing. She snaked her arm though Ross's.

Laura approved wholeheartedly.

Lovers. That's nice. Now we just have to pretend we haven't noticed.

"Mission accomplished then?" Harry asked.

Laura tried to unhear it, but Ross didn't seem at all bothered as he and Amy made a fuss of their returning daughter. Then he picked up a small baby sock from their sun lounger and faced up to Evie in the buggy.

"It's the season's biggest game," he said. "Everything depends on whether goalkeeper Evie can save a penalty. Dad shoots… Evie saves!"

Then he took her from the buggy.

"Now space pilot Evie has to fly to Jupiter!" In an instant, Ross's daughter was on his shoulders leaving the Earth's atmosphere.

"Eee-owwww!" roared Ross.

Evie was wide-eyed with the adventure.

29

A View of the Bay

#39: Jane Fellows

Posted 5 years ago

My sister and I have so many happy memories of childhood holidays in the late '60s, early '70s at Sandy Bay. Just the sight of the first orange coat and we were floating on a cloud. It really was fun all the way. We know Mum and Dad worked hard for the money. Without their determination we wouldn't have made all those unforgettable memories. Thanks from the bottom of our hearts, Mum and Dad. You gave us everything and we will never forget how lucky we were. We girls miss you both xx

Freddie Archer replied 5 years ago

Hello everyone. Freddie here again. What a wonderful post, Jane. The orange coats worked tirelessly to make everyone's stay a memorable one, from morning games with the children right through to late night duties in the ballroom. I applied to be an orange coat at that time with the aim of becoming a children's entertainer, but it wasn't to be. I did work in the bar though, so I may have served your parents. I'm glad you all had such a wonderful time.

*

It was after seven on Friday evening, two and a half hours before the sun would set. The family was seated at a large round table in the busy outdoor area of a restaurant with a view over the still waters of Sandy Bay. Just after the empty plates of their starter course were cleared away, Laura became lost amid the chatter, her gaze beyond them all, out to sea, fixed on the horizon.

Harry, seated next to her, leaned in.

"Now, it might be because I'm forthright, and that's always true after two gin and tonics..." He took a sip from his nearly empty glass. "But you've done well."

"Thanks Harry. Done well at what?"

"Look around Sandy Bay. Look around any place in the world. You'll see millions of families who get on well, have fun, and support each other through thick and thin. This was one of those families until your dad died."

"And then it wasn't?"

"And then it wasn't. But I think now it is. At least it's well on the way. Thanks to you, Laura. You see, families usually rely on one or two strong characters to take the lead. You've done that. You've taken the baton from Bev."

"I think I had a little help from a certain grumbling old step-dad though... who I've never given the affection he deserves, until now. Okay, old friend?"

"I'm good with that, old friend. But there's just one

other thing. Is there a chance you're being completely stupid?"

Laura was a little taken aback.

"How do you mean?"

"Speaking as a friend, I'm not prepared to put up with you staring out to sea for the next couple of days. This is a family holiday not Pirates of the Caribbean."

"You're absolutely right, Harry – you *have* had too much gin and tonic."

"Agreed – but telling yourself you don't care about El Honcho before you've even snogged him…"

"Harry…"

"Can you imagine Humphrey Bogart telling Lauren Bacall he'll Skype her? Go and meet him, Laura. Meet him and get a sense of him up close. See who he is. See if he's a real man or a bloody picture pasted onto the screen. Take a chance."

"It's not that simple."

"From this side of two gins, it looks really easy. You… get… off… your… butt… and… go."

Harry sat back and waved to a waiter for service.

Laura sat back too, but didn't want to drink. She was fighting the feeling that she might be in love. It seemed stupid, immature, juvenile and absolutely bloody ridiculous. She hadn't even held him in her arms. Was she in love? For real? Maybe that thirteen-year-old girl in Manchester, with the benefit of the past year, had discovered the answer.

What would science say? She had googled it, of course, and ended up reading a theory that people don't just fall in love once, but over and over, a little each time, gradually cementing the bonds. Is that how it was with Matt? Only, they hadn't done anything. Not really. Or had they? Reality was messing with her head again.

She stared out to sea. A ferry had appeared on the horizon. Probably headed for France. What would it be like on the ferry home, looking back at the shrinking island? How would she feel?

*

After dinner, Laura left the table to lean against the railing that overlooked the sea. They were due to return home on Monday. Between now and then would be quality time spent with her family. As for Matt… he'd be flying home tomorrow. That much she knew. As for which airport…

Didn't he mention Gatwick?

Whatever stupid idea her brain was trying to conjure up, she stopped it. There was no point seeing this as a last chance to do something, because she didn't want to do anything. She was hardly likely to go to the airport and meet him. After all, would he come to the island to meet her?

Ah, that's exactly what he'd planned to do.

"You're staring out to sea again," said a familiar voice behind her.

"Can't a person stare out to sea without it becoming some kind of metaphor?"

"Not unless they're a coastguard or a lighthouse keeper."

Laura turned to face her step-father.

"I'm fine, Harry."

"Even you don't believe that. You're overstressed, overworked and you don't get to be with your man. Still, they say life isn't fair. And as for love…"

"Haven't you heard? Love is simply the human species protecting itself from extinction via a subconscious process."

"Oh," said Harry. "I can't see anyone putting that on a Valentine's Day card."

"That's what I said!"

"Who to?"

"Someone who'd read a study. According to science, a biological imperative has gone so deep into our brains that we believe love is real, when it's really just chemicals."

"So love is like a tin of paint?"

"Yes, red paint, probably. Full of dopamine, adrenaline and noro-something."

"Ah, that's probably what gives love its sheen."

"Don't worry, Harry. If scientists try to kill off the candlelit dinner, I'll fire a champagne cork to hold them off."

"You wouldn't be alone in that."

"No…" Laura almost laughed, but it transformed into a sigh. "So you think I should do something?"

"Yes, because you're big hearted and you're full of love. I just hope this guy appreciates how lucky he is."

"I'm not so sure Jonathan saw it that way."

"Jonathan was an idiot. You tolerated him for too long because you couldn't stand back far enough to see he was a rocky asteroid and you were the Earth."

"Is this two gin and tonics speaking?"

"Three, but it's in a good cause."

"I know what I need to do, but it's too ridiculous."

"But you're going to do it?"

"I haven't made up my mind."

"You don't have much time."

"I lied to him, Harry, and now I'm being punished for it. The sensible thing to do now is risk making myself look an even bigger idiot – which doesn't sound very sensible."

"If it doesn't work out, I won't tell anyone. Being alone is what's hard. You've been given a chance. Okay, so it's a stupid ultra-modern holiday romance with the guy in the wrong country, but you can't let a little thing like that get in the way."

"I need more time to think."

"You can't stare at the sea forever, Laura. Sometimes you have to get in the boat and set sail."

Harry patted her on the arm and toddled off back to their table.

Laura considered it all.

Everything.

The rocks under their feet dated back billions of years. How many people had come and gone in humankind's brief time standing upon them? Who recalled their names? She thought back to the ancient villa they had visited in Newport. The Beaker people were the first recorded inhabitants there, named after their pottery. Then came the Romans, the Saxons, the Vikings, and the English. Four thousand years of history, of feet upon these rocks, of faces staring out over this sea. And, at some point, Joan and Stan, standing here for their brief time in the sun, full of life and then not existing anymore. And then came Bev and Jim, absolutely blazing with life... for a brief time. And then it was Bev and Harry. Long decades seemingly unending, and yet coming to an end. And now Laura Cass, just another temporary immortal, trying to make her mark. Only she would have to hurry, because Amy and Ross, and even Evie, were waiting for their turn to head into a future that would come and go all too soon.

Laura looked for boats on the horizon. There were none. But Harry was right – life was too short and too precious to do nothing. She needed to do something drastic because the world didn't hand out happiness. Only opportunity. And if she made a fool of herself, who, a billion years from now, would know? Or care?

30

Taking A Chance

#40: Trisha O'Neill

Posted 4 years ago

Where do I start! I was an orange coat back in the Golden Age (1960-66). Long hours? They all joined up! Well, almost. Brekkie started at eight and the ballroom closed at midnight. Phew!

In between it was rigid rules for staff, but not for married male campers with a wandering eye (some had wandering hands too). Also, we had to deal with the emotional disasters of the girls we worked with (usually caused by the boys we worked with – occasionally with serious consequences for the girls if a marriage proposal didn't follow quickly, if you get my meaning). We had a blast though. Such fun and such great friends I made.

It's hard to explain how it felt to be an orange coat on the camp. At the time it was a bit like being a celebrity. Everyone knew you, but you had no time to really get to know them, not with thousands coming to stay every week.

Honestly, it was the best job in the world!

Freddie Archer replied 4 years ago

Hello everyone. Freddie here. Trisha, I salute
you! The orange coats WERE celebrities, and
were the very best of us!

*

It was five a.m. on Saturday and Laura was sipping hot
coffee at the dining table. There was a sense of the
celestial clock counting down the time before they
boarded the ferry home to the mainland on Monday
morning.

Should she text him? Call him?

Yes.

And when should she do this?

Ross came out to use the loo.

"You're up early, Laura?"

"I couldn't sleep."

"Oh. Um... I just wanted to say this holiday... I've
never been on one with all the generations. It's been...
well... really good. Thanks."

"You are so, so welcome, Ross. I hope when you and
Amy move down to the coast, you have the time of your
lives."

"Thanks. I hope you'll come down and see us. You
know, stay over for a few days, a week, whatever's
convenient for you."

"That would be wonderful. Thank you."

"No problem. With the move, we might struggle to
afford holidays for a bit, but when you come to stay, we'll
make that a holiday. You know, seaside walks, restaurants,
the different generations."

"It sounds brilliant. I can't wait."

"Amy thinks you should move down too. To be near us."

"Oh, does she?"

"I think it's a fantastic idea. It's your call, of course. It's an option for you."

"It's the nicest option I've had in a very long time."

She got up and approached him. And for the first time they embraced.

"Thank you, Ross."

"No, thank you, Laura."

They separated.

"I don't suppose Harry mentioned Arnold, did he?"

"Pardon?"

"No, it's okay. Let me finish my coffee – then I have to scoot."

"Where are you going?"

"I'm going... to take a chance."

*

Even though the first sailing wouldn't be for a while, Laura felt bound to be first there. Hopefully there would be no hold-ups. Certainly, drivers had no excuse for being late. Here, you just had to pootle a few miles across a small island. Honestly, if anyone held them up by being late, she would...

She calmed her thoughts and started the engine. The ferry would sail on time. They didn't take into account dim motorists.

She checked her phone. She couldn't text or call, of course. She'd known for a while this simple option wasn't one that was open to her. Everything they had done had been done at a distance. If they were to go forward or break up, she wanted it to be face to face. She wanted to see him in the flesh. Nothing else would do.

She reached the port at half-five. The waiting area wasn't busy yet. It certainly wasn't the most popular time for crossing the sea.

She checked the notice board. Ferries to Lymington sailed hourly. Check-in was thirty minutes before sailing. The first sailing would be at 6.25 a.m.

Noted for her planning instincts, on the million-to-one off chance that she might need it, she had booked a ferry ticket two hours after telling Matt she was a liar, while still slightly drunk and unable to sleep.

Time slowed to a crawl. At one point, she suspected it may have even come to a halt. It did offer plenty of scope for weighing up her situation though.

Too much scope.

Eventually, however, there was activity. Car engines started up and they were moving forward to board the vessel.

Next up, it was the interminable wait for the ferry to leave the dock. That wasn't the half of it though. Once they did set sail, the crossing duration seemed like Earth to Alpha Centauri. Perhaps it was fuel economy. Maybe the boat wasn't under full power, but just drifting because the tide would bring them in at half the cost sometime next week.

In the lounge area, Laura picked up a free magazine. On page five there was a feature on Celebrity Travel, only there didn't seem to be any Isle of Wight ferries involved.

She turned the page.

The next article began with a question. 'What kind of person are you?'

She tried to work out what kind of person she was, because it seemed to be cruel of Nature to have removed her common sense. It was fine for an indecisive teen to act like an indecisive teen, but at fifty-two people were supposed to be wise.

She checked her phone. Nothing from Angela.

Nothing?

At 6.45 on a Saturday morning? Perhaps she'd died.

Laura imagined it. A funeral with texts still coming from the coffin regarding fresh ideas for the website.

She put the magazine down and got real. What if she started her own business? How would that work? Wouldn't it be too many kinds of hell to undertake at fifty-two?

She googled 'how to start your own company'. A lot of business stuff came up, from incorporation to tax rules. She truly didn't fancy having a Day One with all that.

Her phone pinged.

Matt?

It was Angela

*

Driving off the ferry onto the mainland brought it all home. She was heading for Gatwick Airport to meet a man who read stupid science tracts about chemical induced romance.

On the other hand, he was fun to discuss characters in a novel with – and she didn't know anyone else who found that as interesting as she now did.

Oh, and her heart lifted when she was talking with him. That was enough to risk making a fool of herself. She was right to go and meet him face to face and see how it played out. He might not want to take it further. But hey-ho.

The seventy-mile drive through the parched English countryside took time, with a couple of hold-ups on the way. She eventually reached Gatwick at nine.

Having parked the car, she was in the terminal by twenty past. She checked the arrivals board. The only morning flight from Alicante would be landing at 11.30 a.m.

Her phone pinged. It was an email.

Ah, there you are again, Angela.

This definitely couldn't go on. Angela was destroying…

No, it wasn't Angela, it was Laura Cass who was destroying Laura Cass's life.

She took a seat and downloaded a book called 'Starting Your Own Business.'

Time continued to crawl, but she used it well. A while after Matt's flight had landed she had a much better grasp of how people set up their own companies.

She checked her phone. Would he have his baggage by now?

She pulled up his name on her contacts list.

She pressed the call button.

It was ringing.

31

Laura…?

#41: Freddie Archer

Posted 4 years ago

Hello everyone. It's Freddie here again. Lots has happened since I last commented. I hoped the camp would thrive. Now I hear the new owners have changed the name from Martin's back to Hopton's. A nice touch, I'd say. Good luck to all who spend a week or two there. Go and refresh yourselves, restore yourselves, fix what's broken, have fun, and make lots of wonderful memories.

*

Several things flashed through her mind. He lived in Warwick. She lived in London. That was over a hundred miles. The midpoint was Milton Keynes. Warwick had a castle. Holiday romances fade once you're back at work.

"Laura?"

It was him. His voice sounded bright.

Her phone beeped.

"Hi Matt… hang on one sec, I have another call." She switched calls. "Angela, hi. Listen, can you please stop

229

interrupting my holiday? This level of commitment would require me to be made up to a full partner, okay? Goodbye."

She sent Angela's call to hell and reconnected with Matt.

"Sorry, Matt, what is it you want?"

"Um… you called me."

"Oh right… yes, I just wanted to say sorry for the mess up. I'm not used to dealing with men online. Plus I've been getting close to burnout at work. Sorry, do you have time for this call?"

"Tons of time, Laura. I'm actually a lot nearer to you now."

Believe me, I know.

"Oh?"

"I'm at Gatwick waiting for my bags. How's the Isle of Wight?"

"Oh it's… still surrounded by water. That was Angela on the line, by the way, just making sure I don't have any kind of holiday."

"That's not great. Mental health-wise, stress is the curse of the age. It takes a toll in so many ways. Better people than me have written thousands of books on the subject, and yet it seems to be on the increase."

"I'm sorry I lied. That was never in my mind. It was just… well, like stepping into quicksand. I got sucked down into it. I knew what I was doing though. I was stressed, tired and fed up, but in the end I took a risk and failed."

"So what's the situation at work? From what I can see, you could run your own business with no greater degree of stress."

He's still talking to me.

"Yes… yes, it's true I've got the firm a lot of work

though my own efforts. There are clients who only talk to me. Never Angela. I get the feeling some of them don't like her manner."

"You could always consider taking those clients with you. It would certainly give you a good start should you want to go solo in business."

"I don't know. Starting a business sounds like a fast-track ticket to the grave."

"Funny, you should say that – I'm thinking of starting one."

"Oh… well, I'm sure you'll have good days. It's just, for me, I doubt I could…" Her text alert pinged. She checked it. "Oh, actually, I'm joining a partnership with Angela to run the business together."

"Is that true?"

"Of course it's true. Hang on, I'll just reply… I'm saying… we'll hire another member of staff right away."

"You seem to have crazy things happen to you."

"Yes… one second… Angela says we can't afford it. I'm just replying… yes we can, I've been over the figures in the secret files in the secure part of the system."

"Laura… are you for real?"

"Yes, I am, Matt. Really for real. Um, so tell me about living on the Isle of Wight. I don't know much about the real island… the non-tourism island. I used to hear stories about it being the most boring place on earth to grow up. I'm sure that's an exaggeration."

"What can I say? We had the cinema, ice-skating, bowling, swimming in the sea, playing beach football, surfing, canoeing, cycling, forest hikes, sailing. Oh, and diving."

"Okay, so that's not boring."

"I haven't got to the other stuff yet – the music festivals, arts festivals, the decent bars in Newport, Ryde and, of course, Cowes."

"Point taken."

"Sorry, that wasn't fair. Any more texts from Angela?"

"No, she's probably busy hating me."

"Look, maybe we should stay in touch. I mean we're friends, right?"

"Yes," said Laura. "Friends."

Friends…

Was that enough?

She looked down the terminal. Holidaymakers everywhere. There would be holiday romances that would flourish and then fade…

"I'm thinking they'll struggle to just be friends."

"They? Who's they?"

"The characters in the novel I'm pretending to write."

"Okay… have they had any kind of physical involvement yet?"

"No, just video calls, texts and phone calls."

"Oh, you mean like us. Yes, so as friends there could be a lot more to come. For example, in our friendship, I have no idea what you look like from the neck down."

"Would you like to?"

"If it would benefit your fake novel, then, of course."

"What about age? Would that make a difference? In the fake novel, it's possible they might still want a hot relationship even though they've turned fifty."

"Can you give me a minute? I just have to get my bags. I'll call you soon."

"Okay."

She waited. The minutes began to stack up. Lost luggage? A security check? Was Matt a drug mule?

An age passed. A few people emerged. And then more. She scanned them all. And then… a group of middle-aged men, all looking tanned, all looking healthy.

THOSE LAZY, HAZY, CRAZY DAYS OF SUMMER

Is that him?

He looked taller than on the screen. He had to be six-foot-two? She wondered. How would their bodies line up when…?

He's leaving!

"Matt?"

He turned. He stopped. His friends stopped. His face failed to show any degree of understanding… for a moment or two. And then…

"Laura?"

Laura hurried to him. They were reunited. Or at least, united.

They kissed… in her mind's eye.

In reality, he looked completely confused and they shook hands.

32

Look To The Horizon

#42: howardrenshaw

Posted 2 years ago

My dad passed away recently after a long battle with emphysema. I was with him a lot during his final weeks and we'd sit and talk about our family holidays in Sandy Bay back in the 1960s. We were regulars there for twelve summers and I think my dad loved the adventure of going on the ferry. I'm sure he imagined himself as a sea captain off to sail the world! To me, that holiday camp by the bay was like stepping into a different world filled with happiness. I've been to dozens of countries since those far off days and stayed in some of the very best hotels, but nothing, and I do mean absolutely NOTHING compares with those precious weeks at wonderful Sandy Bay with my parents. Thank you with all my heart to my much missed Mum (Dawn) and Dad (Tony) for those wonderful summer holidays. I truly wish I had the power to turn back the clock and experience it all over again with you xx

Freddie Archer replied 2 years ago

Hello everyone. Freddie here. Howard, what a wonderful tribute to your parents and also to Sandy Bay. It warms my heart.

*

Memories were on the breeze swirling around the island-bound ferry. Laura had no idea how this was going to work, but she knew it was more than any kind of summer romance. It had already lasted a lifetime.

"How does it feel to be crossing the sea to the place you grew up?" she asked.

"It always feels just right," said Matt. They were at the bow of the boat, looking ahead.

"You'll see your mum."

"Yes, although I have a week's worth of dirty laundry with me and no fresh clothes. Mum isn't expecting me until Monday…"

"Monday?"

"Ah… yes, I told my mum I'd be there Monday."

"Any reason?"

"There's a local woman from East Cowes… I thought I might try to put things right with her."

Laura smiled. "I feel like we should embrace or something. What do you think?"

"I think we could try."

"Okay."

So they tried. And held on.

It was a few minutes before they spoke again.

"What happened with your dad?" Laura asked.

"He left when I was a baby. I never knew him."

"Have you ever thought of trying to find him?"

"Yes, I've thought about it – but no, I won't. I just think of him as a nice old guy sitting with a glass of beer looking out over the sea and wishing me well."

"That's a nice image."

"It's probably better than the truth, but we'll never know."

"You said we."

"Did I?"

"Were you hoping I'd stick around?"

"Kind of."

"Kind of?"

"Yes, kind of – it's a technical term that means definitely, yes, do not go anywhere, please stick around."

"Do you know how it might work for us? We live in different places."

"We'll find a way."

"That's what I think too. Can you say those words now?"

"The ones you just texted me?"

"Yes."

"The words you've been longing to hear?"

"Yes."

"Okay… would you like strawberry or apricot jam?"

"Mmm, thank you."

The wind flared, sending a fine spray into their faces.

"Look to the horizon," said Laura.

"Is that a romantic thing or just to combat sea-sickness?"

"I'm not sure, but my step-father insists on it."

"And is he a man of great wisdom?"

"Do you know, I think he is."

So they looked to the horizon. And Matt squeezed her hand. And Laura squeezed it back. And in that moment, watching the sunlit island growing in the distance, she knew that the fantasy had ended. That reality had taken over. That, at last, anything was possible.

Epilogue:

A Bench by the Sea

Under a shimmering azure sky, gentle waves lapped against the shoreline, and a sandcastle that had stood since mid-morning was now in peril of a lunchtime disaster. Not that it troubled the boy who had built the fortress. He was urging the waves on to do their work and was only disappointed that they didn't seem too bothered.

Fifty yards behind him, an elderly man with sunglasses and a straw hat took a seat on a promenade bench. He loved the view. The grand vista of the bay, the distant hills rolling down to meet the sea on two sides with water to the horizon in the middle. Then the small waves gently approaching. And the squeals of children paddling and splashing among the tame breakers. Sandcastles, umbrellas, deck chairs, sun loungers, holidaymakers. The smell of sea and sunscreen, and of vinegar on fish and chips. Under the glorious summer sun, everything looked just right.

Not for the first time that day, he took out his phone and checked a particular, seldom used website. The banner notification was unambiguous. 'Due to various factors, this site will be closing soon and will be archived. Thank you for your interest.'

Having finally decided what to say, he typed into his phone.

#43: Freddie Archer

Posted Today 12:35 p.m.

Hello everyone. It's Freddie here again. I see no-one has commented on this thread for a couple of years. I just thought it worth typing one more thing before they close it down. I'm at Sandy Bay right now. First time in many, many years. So many memories. Almost too many to bear. Wherever you are in the world, I wish you well – and if you ever get the chance to visit Sandy Bay, do take it. It really is a magical place.

He closed his phone. Did he believe his own words? That Sandy Bay was a magical place? Yes, he did. After all, how many of its summer visitors had written a fresh chapter into their lives? The number would be close to countless.

"Yay!" cried the five-year-old castle builder. His creation was now a formless mound that would soon vanish altogether. His father wished the credit card bill this holiday had racked up could be pulverized in a similar fashion – and it would, steadily, with overtime at work to make sure they were set fair by Christmas and ready to book another summer break. He smiled at his son and his wife. Life could be good.

Strolling onto the promenade, an elderly woman in a sun hat and sunglasses paused to take in the view. And what a view – utterly perfect on such a glorious day. She looked beyond the squeals of those on the beach and beyond the lapping waves and shallow waters. Her eyes sought distant boats. And there were a few if you looked hard. She loved distant boats with their hint of someone else's exciting adventure.

She considered her own adventure – coming back to the Isle of Wight after the death of her second husband, Bill. It hardly ranked as an adventure, more a routine. She wouldn't come again though. Too many memories. And without Bill to distract her, she had found – somewhat unexpectedly – that those memories took on a greater power to make her feel sad.

Why had she come? She wondered about that. She supposed she wanted to feel again, and being at Sandy Bay certainly did that. She could set aside the darker days of being married to first husband Ralph, who let her down with other women, money, gambling, and drink. Thank God they never had children. Men like Ralph didn't deserve to have children. She wondered briefly – what would they have grown up like?

As an orange coat all those years ago, she had given so much but had received much in return. Of course, the old camp was gone now. She'd been up to the new place for a look around. It bore the name of Hopton's but it seemed to lack something. She supposed it actually lacked nothing but it seemed to offer only the faintest echoes of the life she had enjoyed there.

She felt lonely.

It was a shame she and Bill never had children.

Oh cheer up, Georgie, you silly twit.

She began to hum a song. That had been Bill's thing, to have a song to sing. It would rarely be a song in her heart, but she liked the romanticism of it. Pavarotti and so on. Bill said you could hear the tears rolling down their cheeks. She liked that. He said he saw a photo once, and they did have tears. It was acting, of course. She knew that. The end of La Boheme. Rodolfo and Mimi. Very sad.

She stopped humming and decided it had been a mistake to come to Sandy Bay. The song was over. The tears of Pavarotti and the lady were never real. But the emptiness in her heart was.

She wandered over to a bench. There was man of her own age on the other end, but she said nothing. She preferred to keep herself to herself these days. She would enjoy the view for a few minutes, then she'd go back to the hotel and sit in the cool, air-conditioned shade of the foyer during the hottest part of the day.

Freddie put his phone away. It was time to get going. Sandy Bay had cheered him a little. No, it had cheered him a lot. He wouldn't come again though. Too much trouble. He'd see out the rest of the week and then board Saturday's ferry home. It was only Monday, but he was looking forward to that now.

He smiled as an excited boy left the beach with his parents. They were brushing sand off his feet prior to putting his trainers back on.

"This is the best holiday ever," the boy exclaimed. "Thanks Mum, thanks Dad. And thanks to the orange coats. And thanks to Ross."

Freddie smiled again. It was so good to see kids having the time of their lives. So easy to miss, so easy to overlook, but to Freddie, happy children today would ensure a happier world tomorrow.

With a slight change in the gentle breeze, Georgie got a whiff of something pleasant, if old fashioned. Soap. Obviously, the man on the bench chose to keep himself clean without the need for the millions of products you could buy these days. She liked that.

She got up to go.

But something that local woman, Laura, said came back to her. "Keep life simple. Next time you see a potential Mr Right, just say hello."

Potential Mr Right…?

She almost laughed, but she didn't.

Show a little decorum, old girl. You're a respected senior citizen.

But Laura was right. Funny how being old and on your own could strip away self-confidence. The young Georgie was still in there. Laura had seen that. Locals must see it all. The never-ending A to Z of the summer holidays churning and swirling around their little village by the bay.

Georgie turned to the man in the straw hat.

"Hello," she said.

He nodded, but remained steadfastly facing the sea.

Shy?

She began to close down her thoughts and feelings again – but once more, that local woman Laura got in first. That was the thing about people who worked hard to make sure holidaymakers had a memorable time. They knew a thing or two.

"Nice to see happy children," she added

There was another pause. The sounds of children playing on the beach rose and fell.

"Yes, it is," he finally said, still looking out to sea.

A ball came their way. A girl came running to retrieve it. They watched her race back to the sand to resume her game.

"You won't believe this," the old man said, "but I used to dream of entertaining children."

"Really?"

He turned to face her.

"I once tried for a job at the old Hopton's holiday camp up the road there. Never quite had the confidence,

I suppose. I ended up working in the kitchen and bar."

"You worked there?"

"Yes, '69 to '70."

"So did I. '67 to '70. I was an orange coat."

For both of them, lowering their sunglasses, life seemed to come to a complete standstill.

"Georgie?"

"Freddie?"

In that moment, the entire span of the universe shrank to a seaside bench on the Isle of Wight, and when they cried 'oh my God' in unison, it was as fine as any opera duet. Better, in fact, because the tears were real.

THE END

Thank you for reading Those Lazy, Hazy, Crazy Days of Summer. I hope you enjoyed it as much as I enjoyed writing it. If so, I'd be grateful if you could write a review on Amazon, as I'd love to hear what you think and your feedback is invaluable.

For more information about my latest releases, simply pop over to my website...

www.markdaydy.co.uk

Many thanks,

Mark